THE DIAMOND CAPER

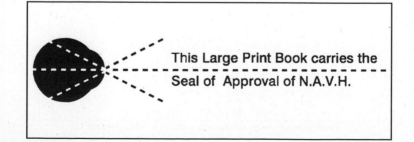

This Large Print Book carries the
Seal of Approval of N.A.V.H.

THE DIAMOND CAPER

PETER MAYLE

THORNDIKE PRESS
A part of Gale, Cengage Learning

Farmington Hills, Mich • San Francisco • New York • Waterville, Maine
Meriden, Conn • Mason, Ohio • Chicago

GALE
CENGAGE Learning®

LIBRARY OF CONGRESS CATALOGING-IN-PUBLICATION DATA

Mayle, Peter.
  The diamond caper / Peter Mayle. — Large print edition.
    pages cm. — (Thorndike Press large print mystery)
    ISBN 978-1-4104-8392-8 (hardback) — ISBN 1-4104-8392-4 (hardcover)
  1. Marseille (France)—Fiction. 2. Large type books. I. Title.
PR6063.A8875D53 2015b
823'.914—dc23   2015034734

Published in 2015 by arrangement with Alfred A. Knopf, a division of Penguin Random House LLC

Printed in Mexico
1 2 3 4 5 6 7 19 18 17 16 15

In memory of dear old Fanny

CHAPTER 1

Why is it that bad news so often arrives on Monday mornings?

The call came at 6:00 a.m. local time, waking a reluctant Elena Morales from a deliciously deep sleep. It was her boss, Frank Knox, founder and CEO of Knox Insurance, and there was an undercurrent of tension in his voice. There was a problem, he said, and it was urgent. Despite the early-morning Los Angeles traffic, Elena was with him in his office by 7:30.

For once, his normally cheerful manner had deserted him. "I guess you've read some of this stuff already," he said, opening the folder of newspaper clippings that was on his desk. "These jewelry robberies in the South of France are getting worse every year. And now it's getting closer to home. A couple of hours ago, I had a call from our Paris office; one of their clients, Madame Castellaci, has just had a bunch of diamonds lifted from her house in Nice. She's hysterical, and the office in Paris has been sent a claim the size of the national debt." He paused to take a swig of coffee.

"What's our liability?" Elena asked.

Knox's eyebrows went up, and he shook his head. "We laid off as much of the risk as we could, but it's still going to hurt us." He took a deep breath. "We're looking at seven figures. Two million, maybe three."

"Do you reckon the claim's valid? What do the police say?"

Knox shrugged. "Not much. From what I've been told, it seems to have been a professional job — no clues, no prints, nothing."

"And what do our people in Paris say?"

"Help."

Knox slumped back in his chair. Elena had never seen him look so despondent. He was planning to retire in a few months and enjoy a prosperous retirement, after thirty-five years of hard work. And now this. Even with the money he'd put away over the years, it was a blow.

"Frank, what do you want me to do?"

"I'd like you to get over to the Paris office and go through everything they know," Knox said after a deep sigh. "And then I'd like you to go down to Nice and grill the client." He held up one hand. "I know, I know. The police will have done that, but sometimes they miss little things. It's a long shot, but it's all we've got." He slid the folder of clippings across the desk. "Here — something to read on the plane. Good luck."

Elena's feelings were mixed as she packed for the trip. Normally, she would be delighted to be going once again to France. This visit, however, was unlikely to offer much in the way of enjoyment. Her colleagues in the Paris office would be distracted and anxious, and if Madame Castellaci in Nice was anything like some of Knox's other clients, she would be bad-tempered and suspicious. Not for the first time, Elena was reminded of the irony of the insurance business. In theory, a mutually beneficial arrangement; in practice, a relationship in which, so often, each side distrusted the other. Cheating, misrepresentation, and blatant dishonesty — she had seen them all.

She tried to close her suitcase. As usual, it was overpacked; as usual, she had to sit on it to close the locks. She looked at her watch, saw that she had ten minutes before the car came to take her to the airport, and decided to call Sam Levitt, her partner in love and other adventures for the past several years. He was in Jamaica, "consulting" for his old friend Nathan, whose business — smuggling Cuban cigars from Jamaica into the U.S. — had run into a spot of trouble with one of the local protection rackets.

"Sam? Can you talk?"

"To you, my love, always." Even his voice sounded suntanned, Elena thought.

"Listen — something's come up at the office. I've got to go to Paris this afternoon, and then Nice. It's a client who's put in a claim for stolen diamonds, and Frank wants me to check things out."

"You want me to come? I'm nearly done here. Another day or two of twisting arms and kissing ass should do it. Why don't we meet in Marseille? I'll call Francis and tell him to expect us." Their good friend Francis Reboul had been a generous host over the years, and he was always happy to see them.

"That would be great. God, am I sick of the insurance business."

There was a pause before Sam's reply. "Give it up. Send me out to work and become a lady of leisure."

Elena was prevented from pursuing this seductive suggestion by the arrival of the driver. "Got to go. I'll call you from Paris."

In the car, she went over their brief conversation. Was Sam serious? She wasn't always sure. He had wanted her to come down to Jamaica with him, but work had made that impossible, a disappointment for them both. One day soon, she promised herself, you've got to get a life. A new life. According to Air France, she had ten hours and forty-five minutes to think about it before arriving in Paris.

As a small consolation, she was in business class. Comfortable surroundings and a decent glass of chilled Chablis restored her spirits enough to do a little homework, and she opened the folder of clippings that Frank Knox had given her.

The thefts were listed in chronological order, starting in 2002 with a relatively modest haul, valued at three million euros, from a jeweler in Cannes. In 2005, two million from a jeweler in Saint-Tropez. In 2009, fifteen million from Cartier in Cannes. In 2010, seven million from a jewelry wholesaler near Marseille. In 2013, a million from the safe in a Cannes hotel bedroom, a two-million-euro necklace stolen during a celebrity party at the Cannes Film Festival, and, to top them all, one hundred and three million from an exhibition of "Extraordinary Diamonds" in, yet again, Cannes. Elena was shaking her head in disbelief as she put down the folder. All that money for fragments of what one article had described as metastable allotropes of carbon.

Much to Sam's relief, Elena's taste in jewelry was limited to Mexican silver and old gold. She had seen far too many diamond necklaces on the wattled necks of elderly socialites, and this had effectively cured her of diamond envy. As she had once said to Sam, she would prefer to put that kind of money into something practical, like a town house in Paris and a Bentley. Or the house they had seen on their last visit to Marseille. A friend of Francis Reboul's had shown it to them: it was small, built in the early 1920s, and perched on a spur of rock. They had instantly fallen in love with it. The sweeping view of the Mediterranean was enough on its own, but there were other attractions. It was a short and picturesque walk from Reboul's home at Le Pharo, and an even shorter stroll would take them to the delights of Le Petit Nice, whose three Michelin stars made it Marseille's most decorated restaurant.

The asking price for the house was, as Sam had said, enough to make a billionaire's

12

eyes water. But they had to have it. Sam raided what he called his slush fund, Elena sold her stocks, and long-distance negotiations between L.A. and the owner's lawyer in Marseille began. And continued. And went on. And on. The problem was that the proprietor, a seventy-five-year-old widow from Paris, had thought it necessary to obtain the agreement of her extended family to the sale. Children had to be consulted. Grandchildren had to be considered. Even cousins, who under French law might have had some distant claim to the proceeds, could not be ignored. Back and forth went proposals and counterproposals between members of the family until Elena and Sam had almost given up.

A ray of hope had finally come the previous week in the form of a letter from the owner's lawyer. It was possible that the sale could proceed as soon as he had received written confirmation he was awaiting from the family that the sale would not provoke legal complications. Sam had called Reboul with the news, and he had agreed to contact the lawyer and try to move things along. And that was where the matter stood, promising but unresolved.

Thoughts of the house turned to thoughts of the future. A place in Marseille, however idyllic it might be, was of little use to someone who was stuck in a Los Angeles office. Elena had often wondered how long she could put up with her job, even though it paid very well. These last two years, she would have left several times had it not been for her loyalty to Frank Knox. Now that he was retiring, Elena could leave with a clear conscience. Yes, she thought, Frank's retirement was definitely a signal for action. She closed her eyes and lay back in her seat, her head filled with thoughts of life with the Mediterranean as a neighbor.

CHAPTER 2

Ariane Duplessis, president of the Knox Paris office, was waiting in the reception area to welcome Elena with two perfunctory air kisses and a somber expression.

"It was good of you to get here so quickly. Come — the others are in the conference room."

As Elena followed Madame Duplessis down the corridor, she studied the slim figure ahead of her: thick, fashionably cut gray hair, a long cream silk scarf draped across the shoulders, a dark-gray flannel suit, high heels. Business might be going to take a tumble, thought Elena, but, this being France, a high level of chic must always be maintained. She sighed. The meeting was likely to be long and probably very depressing.

There were three men around the conference table, equipped with neat piles of documents and grave faces.

"OK," said Elena, "tell me the worst."

And they did. It seemed that the Castella-cis had always paid their premiums promptly, which ruled out any hope of invalidating their policy. According to their sworn statement, they had taken all the necessary precautions before leaving their house on the evening of the robbery: the alarm system had been activated, the front door double-locked, the window shutters bolted. There were no signs that the wall safe had been forced, and the oil painting concealing the safe had been rehung.

"If that's all true," said Elena, "they're pretty well covered. What about the police report?"

Madame Duplessis shrugged. "Nothing. No fingerprints, no clues. *Hélas,* the thief didn't leave his address."

The rest of the afternoon was spent going through the insurance policy, line by line, seeking to find an escape clause that would stand up in court. But finally, Elena had to admit that they had come up against a dead end.

Madame Duplessis walked her back to the elevator. "It doesn't look so good, does it?"

Elena shook her head. "Unless I can find something when I see the Castellacis in Nice, I guess we're going to have to pay up."

On her way back to the hotel, Elena noticed that it was nearly 6:00 p.m. in Paris; that would be around noon in Jamaica. She'd call Sam, and then have a drink. Or maybe not: after the lousy day she'd had, she'd have a drink and then call him.

Whenever she stayed at the Montalembert, she felt herself relaxing as soon as she set foot in the lobby. The people were charming, the bar was inviting, and the prompt arrival of a glass of Champagne began to lift her spirits. She settled back, and called Jamaica.

"Sam, I need cheering up."

"That bad, was it?"

"I've had more fun at a wake. The clients are on the phone every day, screaming for their check, and the police have nothing to go on — no prints, no forced entry, no clues. So right now, it feels like a wasted trip."

"Do you know them, the clients?"

"No. Why do you ask?"

"Well, if there's no evidence of forced entry, if everything's as neat and tidy as they say, one obvious possibility is that it was an inside job. It's been known to happen. So I guess the first thing to do is meet the clients and get some idea of what kind of people they are."

"I know. That's my next stop."

"Oh, I spoke to Francis, and he's expecting you in Marseille. Just call and tell him when. I'll be there in a couple of days. By the way, where are you?"

"In the bar at the Montalembert."

"Good girl. Don't talk to any strange men, OK? And try not to worry. I miss you."

The next morning, having slept off most of her jet lag and treated herself to the indulgence of breakfast in bed with croissants and *café crème,* Elena took the forty-five-minute flight down to Marseille. After the drab gray overcast of Paris, the Provençal sky seemed almost shockingly blue. She had reached the arrival hall and was digging around in her handbag for her sunglasses when she heard someone call her name.

And there was her host, Francis Reboul, tanned and dapper in his pale linen suit, along with his chauffeur, Olivier. After enthusiastic embraces had been exchanged, Elena and Reboul waited outside in the sun for Olivier to bring the car around.

"I have some excellent news, my dear." Reboul took an envelope from his pocket and passed it to Elena. "This is from my new best friend, the *notaire* who is dealing with your house. Everything is settled, and the sale can now go through. Congratulations!"

"Francis, that's wonderful. I didn't know that you and the *notaire* were friends. How did that happen?"

"I asked him to come to Le Pharo, gave him a grown-up serving of *pastis, et voilà.* I suggested that he tell his client in Paris that you had become impatient, and were considering other properties. That, and another *pastis,* seemed to do the trick."

Elena leaned over to kiss him. "You're a star — I'm thrilled. I can't wait to tell Sam."

In the car going back to Le Pharo, Reboul was silent and pensive for a few moments, as though considering an important decision. When he spoke, it was little more than a chauffeur-proof whisper.

"I've been invited to this party," he said, "by my old friend Tommy Van Buren, who I met when we were students at Harvard. A couple of years ago, he bought a property outside Cannes, and the party is to celebrate the finish of the renovation work. And this is where I need a little moral support." He looked at Elena, eyebrows raised, brow furrowed.

"Of course," said Elena. "I'm great at moral support. Ask Sam."

Reboul smiled, and patted her hand. "My

problem is that the architect, who's also the decorator, will undoubtedly be there — a lady named Coco Dumas. Some years ago we had a relationship, which unfortunately ended badly. To be honest, I would much prefer not to go to the party." He paused, and shrugged. "But I don't want to disappoint my old friend. And so I'm wondering if you would come with me to provide — how can I put it? — some social cover." It was Elena's turn to pat his hand. "Don't worry. I'm good at social cover, too. When are we going?"

"Tomorrow."

Over dinner that evening, Reboul was more forthcoming about his reluctance to go to the party. Some of the story Elena already knew, or suspected. He had been married to a woman named Mireille, whom he adored. She died young, of cancer, and Reboul — rich, and suddenly on his own — had become an unwilling eligible bachelor. Over the years there had been several liaisons, most of which had ended amicably, until Reboul and Coco had met at a cocktail party. She was good-looking and amusing, he was lonely, and one thing led to another. But, to Coco's disappointment, it didn't look as though it was leading up the aisle to a permanent position as the second Madame Reboul. No matter how many hints she dropped, Reboul preferred to remain single. Coco's disappointment turned to anger, and after one final explosive row, the relationship was over.

"So you can see why I'm not looking forward to tomorrow night," said Reboul. He smiled and shrugged. "Although Tommy tells me she's done a spectacular job with the house." He looked at his watch. "And now, my dear, I think an early night would do you a lot of good. That flight from Los Angeles takes some time to get over."

The evening sun was just starting its slide into the Mediterranean when Elena and Reboul left the *autoroute* and headed for the hills, making their way through the tangle of suburban roads behind Cannes. Elena was looking at the gas stations and nondescript storefronts and billboards advertising Orangina and the local supermarket. "Seems like an awful long way from the Cannes Film Festival," she said. Reboul smiled and nodded. "It gets better."

They turned off the main road, passed under a stone bridge, and were now on a narrower road that climbed up into the hills, finally coming to a small gatehouse next to a barred entrance. A uniformed guard came out to the car, checked their names against his clipboard, saluted, and waved them through. "There are a dozen houses on the estate," said Reboul. "Each of them set on about ten acres of land, and all of them with a fantastic view. You'll see."

In fact, the view was what Van Buren had bought. It was a long, curving panorama that extended along the coastline from Cannes in the east toward Saint-Tropez in the west. The house had been less impressive — a squat pink concrete barracks, devoid of charm or architectural interest. But that was before Coco Dumas got her hands on it.

The transformation was astonishing. Two wings had been added, and the roofline lowered. Windows had been enlarged, and the complexion of the building had been changed from pink to the color of faded limestone that looked as though it had weathered two hundred years of sunshine. The interior, originally a clutter of poky dark rooms, had been gutted and replaced by space and light. All this had taken nearly two years and had cost several million euros, but Van Buren was delighted with it, and it was one more elegant feather in Coco Dumas's cap.

Even before their car had reached the end

of the pale gravel drive, it was obvious that this was no ordinary house. It glistened in the dusk, the courtyard lit by flaming torches, while white-coated figures moved among the groups of guests, making sure that nobody went thirsty.

Elena and Reboul paused at the entrance to the courtyard to watch the last glow left by the sunset over the Mediterranean, and the glitter of lights along the Croisette, the boulevard that follows the coastline of Cannes for two kilometers. A magical sight.

"And you thought you had the best view in France. You have to admit this ain't bad." It was their host Tommy Van Buren, burly and smiling, the deep tan of his face set off by hair that was almost as white as his dinner jacket. He hugged Reboul and kissed Elena's hand before taking them into the courtyard, where a waiter met them with two glasses of Champagne. But before they had much of a chance to talk, another couple arrived and Van Buren excused himself.

Elena started to take a look, as discreetly as she could, at the women among the other guests. They were an attractive bunch, she thought, smart without being overdressed, and she was about to suggest to Reboul that they join one of the groups when she became aware that she was being watched.

"I get the feeling someone is checking us out," she said. "Over there by the fountain — the woman in the black silk suit."

Reboul looked across the courtyard. "Ah," he said. "That's her. Coco." He sighed, and squared his shoulders. "Do you mind if we get this over with?"

As they were crossing the courtyard, Coco moved away from the group she was chatting with and aimed a wide (and, Elena thought, transparently fake) smile at them. She was in her midforties, with a slender body that had obviously spent many hours in the gym, glossy black hair, and lightly tanned skin. But what made her face memorable were the eyes. They were turquoise. The overall effect, Elena had to admit, was stunning.

"So. Francis. How nice." Coco tilted her head to receive the obligatory cheek-kissing. "Tommy told me you might come. Now, you must introduce me to your friend." She turned to Elena, smiling and extending a scarlet-tipped hand while giving Elena's dress a swift, appraising examination. "What an unusual color," she said. "How brave of you to wear it. Tell me — how did you two meet?"

"It was in Los Angeles," said Elena. "Francis had some business with a friend of mine." She gave Reboul's arm a proprietorial squeeze, and saw Coco's smile falter. Round one to me, she thought.

She was saved from further verbal fencing by Van Buren, who had made his way to the center of the courtyard, borrowed a spoon from a passing waiter, and was tapping the rim of his glass for silence.

"OK, everyone. First, I want to thank you all for being here tonight." He raised his glass to his guests. "I hope this house will see you come back often, and I thought you might like to see what you'd be coming back to. So I managed to persuade Coco, who put it all together, to give you a guided tour." He raised his glass again, this time to her. "Over to you, Madame Architect."

Led by Coco, who gave a running commentary in both French and English, the guests were taken through the house, making appropriately complimentary noises as the various architectural triumphs and decorative touches were pointed out, with a charming mixture of pride and modesty, by Coco.

Elena and Reboul brought up the rear, taking their time to appreciate what had been done. Elena, as she was about to acquire a property herself, was fascinated, taking photographs with her phone of everything from the old stone fireplaces to the sleek granite work surfaces of the kitchen, from lighting fixtures to shutters to the polished concrete of the floors. "She's done a great job, Francis, don't you think? The layout works, and the colors she's chosen are just right." *Click click click* went the phone as more photographs were taken. "I'm impressed."

Reboul nodded. "She has a good eye, and Tommy's the perfect client. He has excellent taste and he's happy to let her do what she wants. And he's obviously delighted with the result. See him over there? He's like a dog with two tails. Let's go over and congratulate him."

They spent a pleasant ten minutes with Van Buren before Reboul saw Coco coming over to join them. He looked at his watch and, with a start, reminded Elena of their plans to meet friends for dinner in Cannes.

On their way back to the car, Elena was frowning. "You didn't tell me we had a dinner date."

"We don't. You'll have to forgive me, but I don't think I could have handled the rest of the evening dealing with Coco. She still makes me a little uncomfortable. I hope you understand."

Elena laughed. "Of course. She's a piece of work. You know what? I wouldn't be surprised if there was something going on between her and Tommy. Women sense these things."

Reboul was silent for a moment. Like him, Tommy was wealthy, and a bachelor. "Not this time, I'm afraid," he said with a smile. "I've known Tommy for nearly forty years, and I can tell you he's not a ladies' man."

CHAPTER 3

The day after the party, Coco Dumas was taking a meeting in her apartment in the Hotel Le Negresco in Nice, a landmark since 1912 on the Promenade des Anglais. It had been built by Henri Negresco, a Romanian businessman who had spared no expense. Among many other decorative touches throughout the hotel, there is an astonishing Baccarat chandelier, with 16,309 crystals, that had been commissioned by Czar Nicholas II. Alas, the small matter of the October Revolution had prevented its delivery.

Coco's meeting took place on her terrace. Her business manager, Gregoire, was at her side, opposite James and Susie Osborne, a young English couple who had sold their Internet business for a great deal of money — "squillions," as Susie said — and were now having fun spending it. Their current project was the renovation of a fine old mansion they had bought on Cap d'Antibes. A friend in Monaco had put them in touch with Coco, and they were here to see what she liked to call her new business presentation.

Gregoire, a dark, precisely dressed young man with a rugby player's physique and broken nose, opened the proceedings by removing his sunglasses to deliver a cautionary tale. It was an unfortunate fact of life these days, he said, that many architects, not content with their legitimate fees, expected to receive kickbacks from their suppliers. Carpenters, plumbers, stonemasons, electricians — it was the same for all of them: they had to pay up if they wanted to stay on the job. Consequently, their prices to the client went up to help cover the bribes. Gregoire shook his head sadly, and paused to let this shocking revelation sink in.

Luckily, he said, chance had brought them to the Cabinet Dumas, an oasis of financial rectitude that was well known along the coast for never demanding any inducements from suppliers. In fact, Coco had gained a reputation for this, something that could be verified by asking any of her clients. The Osbornes nodded their approval, and Gregoire went on to explain the Dumas terms of business before handing over to Coco for the creative part of the presentation.

She had on the table half a dozen leather-bound albums — one for each of the properties she had worked on over the past few years. Each album contained a "before and after" photographic record of the transformations she had achieved, from Marseille to Monaco, and it quickly became clear that the Osbornes liked what they saw. Susie was particularly vocal, finding things that were, in her words, fabulous or awesome on almost every page. They were also impressed to hear that Coco prided herself on taking care of every detail, no matter how tiny: positioning a bidet so that it had a sea view, installing eye-level dishwashing machines to do away with the need to crouch, using slip-proof marble for the shower floors — those small but important touches that are so often neglected. The compliments came in an enthusiastic torrent, Coco was the essence of charm, and Gregoire sent the three of them off to lunch confident that the Cabinet Dumas was about to add to its client list.

The British Airways flight from Jamaica's Norman Manley Airport to Gatwick took off on the dot of 5:50 p.m. Once on board,

Sam collapsed into his seat with the relieved sigh of a man who had survived a hectic week at the office. It could have been a difficult few days, but it was saved by the unexpected rapport that Sam had established with Clyde Braithwaite, who ran several of Kingston's most efficient protection rackets. When he discovered that Sam lived in Hollywood's Chateau Marmont (Sam neglected to tell him it was a hotel) he was impressed at having met one of L.A.'s most distinguished residents. The rum had flowed, generous helpings of jerk chicken had been consumed, and the two men had reached a mutually profitable understanding that was acceptable to both Braithwaite and Sam's friend Nathan, the cigar smuggler. Sam's reward was everlasting gratitude, a handsome check, and a regular supply of Bolívar Belicosos Finos, the ultimate Havana.

It was off-season in Jamaica, and business class was pleasantly uncrowded. For Sam, long-distance flights had always provided a welcome chance to think, as he found it easy to resist the dubious allure of airline food and airline movies. He settled back and considered his most recent conversation with Elena. She had clearly been extremely frustrated by her meeting in Paris. Her

French colleagues had done their home-work, both with their client and with the police. But the thief had given them nothing to work with, and they were left with an empty safe, no clues, and no ingenious theories. It was a situation that piqued Sam's curiosity, and he decided to put himself forward as Elena's unofficial technical adviser. Helping out on the side of law and order would make a change from doing deals for a cigar smuggler, and change was what made Sarn's professional life interesting.

It had been many years since boredom and an increasing resentment at having to get up early had made him resign from a well-rewarded job on Wall Street, and he had since made some unorthodox career moves. Some of these, as he would cheerfully admit, were not quite legal. But he had developed a comfortable relationship with criminal activity as long as it involved intelligence rather than violence. And before too long, outwitting crooks had turned into a lucrative hobby.

As the view from his seat changed color from Caribbean blue to Atlantic gray, Sam's thoughts turned to his last trip to Marseille — a trip that had ended with him flat on his face, feigning death, in the Corsican countryside. He smiled at the memory. This visit, he was sure, would be less eventful. From what Elena had told him, the robbery had been a thoroughly professional job, and by now the stolen diamonds would undoubtedly be in Antwerp, where they would be reworked and given a new identity. Effectively, the originals would have ceased to exist.

Sam rubbed his eyes and yawned. He was still feeling the effects of a little too much Jamaican rum, and sleep came easily.

Elena, in the cheerful company of Reboul's chauffeur, Olivier, was on her way to Nice to see Madame Castellaci, the victim of the diamond robbery. Elena's years in the insurance business had drastically reduced her capacity for optimism, and she didn't hold out much hope of discovering anything that the police had failed to discover; but, as Frank Knox had said, all the boxes had to be ticked. What a waste of a beautiful day.

For Olivier, however, it promised to be anything but wasted. Elena had told him to take the afternoon off, and he had arranged an assignation. He had a seemingly endless supply of aunts scattered along the coast, and, in his words, he liked to keep in touch with them. The two aunts that Elena had met on previous trips had been strikingly good-looking young women, and she had no doubt that this would be another one. How Olivier managed to juggle them all was one of life's minor mysteries.

By the time they had worked their way through the clogged Nice traffic it was too late for anything more ambitious than a quick café lunch. Elena sent Olivier on his way, and she took a table in the sun, a glass of *rosé,* and a *salade niçoise* while she went over what she knew about the Castellacis. Madame and her husband, Ettore, a linguine tycoon from Milan, had what they called a simple holiday home — an Art Deco house overlooking the sea on the Promenade des Anglais. In fact, Elena could almost see it from the café where she was sitting. According to the Paris office, Madame Castellaci was pleasant enough, but her husband was someone whom Ariane Duplessis had described as a tiresome little man, prickly and self-important. Elena hoped that he had vital linguine business to attend to that afternoon, as she tried to summon up some enthusiasm about the meeting. But she gave up. She had to admit that the insurance business had lost any interest it might once have had for her. This visit, for instance, seemed like a total waste of time. What was she likely to find that a thorough police search had overlooked? What was she looking for?

On the short stroll from the café to the Castellaci house, Elena seemed to see nothing but people on vacation, having a good time. Sunglasses, shorts, and summer dresses were the uniform of the day, making her feel completely out of place in her business black. As she reached the Castellaci house, she braced herself and practiced her smile before ringing the doorbell. The peephole in the door slid aside, an eye inspected her, and the door opened to reveal a uniformed maid, who led her into the living room and left to fetch Madame Castellaci.

She was a plump, well-preserved woman, swathed in sky-blue chiffon and wearing, as Elena immediately noticed, an elaborate diamond necklace, which she couldn't help but comment on.

"Ah yes," said Madame Castellaci, "it's all that's left — the only piece the thief didn't get, because I was wearing it that night. Now I never take it off except in bed, when I put it under the pillow." She beckoned Elena to follow her and led the way into the sitting room. From there, they made a brief tour of the house, with madame pointing

35

out the sturdy window shutters and the alarm system, finally removing the oil painting in the bedroom of her husband's grandfather to reveal the wall safe. "There," she said. "That's where they were."

"It's American, top quality, with a million possible combinations." She tapped in a series of figures and opened the door. "You see? No signs of anyone trying to force the lock." She turned toward Elena, wiping her eyes with a handkerchief, a picture of distress. "We thought everything was safe."

Elena was still searching for a suitable reply when Signor Castellaci appeared from his study at the top of the house, bristling with indignation. "Finally you come," he said. "I hope you've brought your checkbook. I've just been speaking with my lawyer in Milan. We've been over everything. The premium — a small fortune — was paid on time. The police have made their investigation. So where is my check? My lawyer wants to know what the problem is. So do I. Well?" He stood in front of Elena on tiptoe, still a few inches shorter than her, his body rigid with anger. "Well?"

All good insurance executives are adept at finding reasons not to pay up, or at least to delay that painful moment for as long as possible. Elena was usually able to make this a little more palatable to her clients by using her natural charm and her genuine sympathy at their loss. But not this time. Try as she might to convince Castellaci of the need to check and double-check every possibility, he continued to fume as he followed her around the house, yapping at her heels like an outraged Pekinese. Lawsuits were mentioned, not once, but several times. Madame Castellaci was in tears. Elena felt like joining her. Finally, after a couple of fruitless hours, even Castellaci had run out of invective, and Elena was permitted to leave, promising to do what she could.

She went back to the café, ordered a coffee, called Olivier and asked him to come and pick her up. When he arrived, slightly disheveled and smiling, she took one look at him and tapped the side of her neck with one finger. "Your aunt," she said. "She's left something on your neck. Looks like lipstick."

Hot, tired, and longing for a shower after the drive back to Marseille, Elena opened the door of the guest suite at Le Pharo and, in an instant, felt the cares of the day melt away. There was a man in her bed. His head was covered by the pillow, with one long arm dangling over the edge of the bed.

Coming closer, she lifted the pillow, saw Sam's tanned, unshaven face, and kissed him on the nose. One eye opened. Half-grinning, half-yawning, Sam patted the side of the bed. "Care to join me?"

CHAPTER 4

"Sam, I can't believe it — I forgot to tell you." Slightly late and slightly flushed, they were on their way down to join Reboul for dinner when Elena stopped at the top of the stairs. "It's the house. They've finally agreed to sell it, thanks to Francis."

Sam picked her up, whirled her around, and kissed her before putting her down. "That's wonderful. What did he do?"

"I think he got their *notaire* drunk, and told him that we were looking around at other places. The owner's coming down from Paris in the next few days to sign all the papers. Isn't that great?"

"It certainly is. You know something? That's going to make you a *châtelaine.*"

"Will I like that?"

"Sure you will. It means you're the lady of the manor. I'll get some T-shirts printed."

Reboul was waiting for them on the terrace, busy with corkscrew and ice bucket.

He looked up and smiled when he saw two beaming faces. "I can see that you've told Sam the good news." He came over and kissed Sam on each cheek. "So you're my new neighbors. Congratulations — I think that house will make you both very happy."

Elena and Sam toasted Reboul, and they all toasted the house, life in Provence, and the joys of friendship before Reboul proposed one final toast to the last of the season's asparagus, which was to be the main event of a light supper. "And with the asparagus," said Reboul, "we shall have one of Alphonse's special treats — a *sauce mousseline,* the undisputed queen of the mayonnaise family. If you ask him nicely, he might even tell you how to make it."

Alphonse had been the chef at Le Pharo for many years, during which time, so Reboul said, he had never been seen without his apron. A rotund, jolly man, he was passionate about eating according to the seasons. Not surprisingly, he was an enthusiastic supporter of a growing movement in France, perhaps one day a law, that would oblige all restaurants to declare anything on their menus that had been deep-frozen and reheated. "That," he was fond of saying, "would sort out the chefs from the amateur firemen."

Alphonse was hovering — if such a solid figure could be said to hover — as they took their places at the table.

"Now then, Alphonse," said Reboul, "what's all this? You said it was just asparagus, but the table is laid for a feast."

"Oh, but Monsieur Francis, man does not live by asparagus alone." Alphonse beamed, and patted his stomach. "And so we have a little fish to follow — *daurade,* caught this morning and served with new peas and those baby potatoes that you like — and then, of course, cheese. And to finish I have made *panna cotta*" — a brief pause here while Alphonse kissed his fingertips — "topped with a layer of liquid caramel, lightly salted, *bien sûr.*"

Alphonse clapped his hands, and his young assistant, Maurice, came out with the asparagus and, quivering with promise in a deep white bowl, the *sauce mousseline.* It was thick — so thick that the silver serving spoon that Alphonse plunged into it remained upright.

"You see?" he said. "That is the test of a true Provençal *mousseline.*" With the care of a surgeon performing a delicate operation, he arranged asparagus and sauce on their plates, wished them *bon appétit,* and bustled back to the kitchen.

After a short period of devotion to the creamy excellence of the sauce, Reboul broke the silence. "Right. Now I want to hear what you two have been doing. Sam, how was Jamaica? I've never been there."

"It was fine." Sam's account of his trip, interrupted by a second helping of asparagus, took them through to the next course, and then it was Elena's turn.

"Well," she said, "I don't want to spoil a lovely evening, so I'll spare you the details of my totally useless visit to see those robbery victims in Nice. Let's just say it wasn't much fun. The wife was in tears, the husband was a little pain in the ass, and I spent the whole afternoon finding absolutely nothing." She shrugged. "So I guess Knox will just have to pay up."

Reboul was frowning. "No clues? No damage? No signs of breaking in?"

Elena shook her head. "Nothing. They gave me a copy of the police report, but it's way beyond my level of French."

"Why don't I ask Hervé to take a look at it?"

Hervé, who had been a friend of Reboul's ever since they had discovered a mutual interest in fine wines and Marseille's soccer team, was a senior figure in the city's police force.

"Won't he have seen it already?"

Reboul laughed. "My dear Elena. What you must remember is that Marseille and Nice might as well be two different countries, each with its own police force. So I'd be surprised if that report has been anywhere near Hervé. Let me show it to him, and see what he thinks."

The evening ended, as so many other evenings had ended, with a nightcap on the terrace, the velvet sky above, the dark, tranquil expanse of the Mediterranean stretching below them.

"This is heaven," said Elena.

Reboul laughed. "It's a good thing you like it, because you're going to have just about the same view. That reminds me — I must call the *notaire* tomorrow to see if we can set a date for the signing. Luckily, from what he's said, it should be pretty straightforward."

"Is that unusual?"

"It depends. Sometimes the seller wants a chunk of the sale price in cash, to reduce taxes. It's illegal, of course, but it happens. And when it does, there's this ritual dance — we call it *la valse des notaires* — just before the actual signing. Obviously, the *notaire,* being a man of the law, can't be

43

involved in anything improper, so when the moment comes to sign, he has to take a call in another office. Or go to the bathroom. Or whatever — the important thing is that he's not present when the cash is checked and counted."

Sam was grinning. "So how does he know when to come back?"

"Well, you can count a lot of cash in five minutes. If it needs to be longer, a hint will be dropped. Anyway, you won't have to worry about all that. The owner has said that she'll be quite happy with a check." Reboul stood up, yawned, and stretched. "I'll call the *notaire* in the morning."

It was a call with surprisingly rapid results. The owner, having procrastinated and dithered for several months, was now anxious to sign as quickly as possible, for fear of losing the sale. "I don't know exactly what the *notaire* told her," said Reboul as he put down the phone, "but it was certainly effective. She's taking the train down from Paris tonight, and the signing has been scheduled for 10:30 tomorrow morning."

Elena and Sam went to meet with the manager of Reboul's bank, who had been called in to supervise the transfer of funds from Los Angeles dollars to Marseille euros.

Naturally, the manager told them, with such a substantial sum, certain safeguards had to be observed before a certified check could be issued: passports had to be produced, studied, and photocopied. A receipt, in triplicate, had to be signed and witnessed. No "i" remained undotted. But eventually, with the certified check folded and stowed safely in Elena's handbag, they were able to have a celebratory glass of Champagne in one of the bars overlooking the Vieux Port.

"Now I know what it's like to be arrested," Elena said. "I was half-expecting them to take my fingerprints. I almost felt guilty when they gave us the check."

Sam raised his glass. "Here's to domestic bliss. Are you excited?"

"I know we're going to love it. But Sam — we're going to want to spend a lot of time here."

"That's the general idea, isn't it?"

"Sure. It's just that if we do, I'll have to quit my job."

Sam leaned forward and took Elena's hand. "Listen to me. You haven't been happy in that job for the past couple of years. It's time to move on. Like I said, you can send me out to work. We'll get by."

Elena's eyebrows went up. "Mr. Levitt, are you suggesting that I should become a kept woman?"

Sam beamed. "You bet. Another glass of Champagne?"

The final nail in the coffin of Elena's insurance career came that evening, in the form of a call from Frank Knox in Los Angeles. After questioning her, more in hope than expectation, to hear what she had discovered, there were a few moments of silence before Frank spoke again.

"I'm sorry about this, but I need you back here right now to help us tie everything up. Just for a couple of days."

There were sighs from Elena and more apologies from Frank before it was agreed — as soon as the signing was completed, Elena would take the shuttle to Paris to pick up the flight to L.A. And on that flight, she promised herself, she'd write her letter of resignation.

CHAPTER 5

Reboul had offered to go with Elena and Sam to the signing — for moral support, so he said, with perhaps a little interpreting on the side. And so, promptly at 10:30, the three of them presented themselves at the offices of Maître Arnaud, in a well-worn building in the 6th arrondissement, a neighborhood favored by several of Marseille's army of *notaires.* A secretary showed them into the waiting room — dark and cramped, equipped with half a dozen hard chairs and a selection of magazines that dated back several years.

Elena was leafing through an ancient copy of *Paris Match.* "Do you think these guys ever wait in their own waiting rooms?"

Reboul smiled. "It's an old tradition. If it looked like they had money to spend on modern waiting rooms with comfortable furniture, their clients would think they were charging too much." He shrugged.

"I've seen worse."

They were warned by an approaching cough. The door opened, and there was Maître Arnaud himself, a large, untidy man with a large, untidy moustache and impressively overgrown eyebrows, smiling and apologetic as he explained that he had been detained by a phone call. "But all is well," he said. "Madame Colbert has recovered from her voyage down from Paris, and she's waiting for us."

He led the way to his office. Clutter had been allowed to flourish there unchecked, with every surface hidden beneath piles of documents and reference books. An oasis of order had been created to accommodate a semicircle of chairs precisely arranged in front of Arnaud's desk, and Madame Colbert had already installed herself in the central, and thus most important, chair.

She was small, birdlike, neatly dressed, and carefully made up. As Elena, Sam, and Reboul were introduced, she inclined her head and smiled, but kept her hands clasped over the ivory handle of her walking stick. Arnaud settled himself behind his desk and separated one pile of documents from the rest. He cleared his throat.

There followed a long, dreary hour and a half of his monotone as he read aloud through every line of the sale documents, pausing occasionally to cock his eyebrows at Reboul to confirm that this vital information was being heard and, with a bit of luck, understood. On and on it went, with Elena and Sam nodding wisely from time to time while Madame Colbert remained motionless and impassive. Finally, Arnaud was finished. The sale documents could be signed — on every page, naturally — and the certified check could be closely scrutinized by Madame Colbert. A bunch of rusting keys was handed over, and Elena and Sam were the proud owners of a house in Provence.

Reboul had insisted that there was only one suitable way to celebrate the occasion: lunch. Lunch in their new home-town, overlooking the Mediterranean. And so he had made reservations at Chez Marcel, a restaurant with, as Reboul put it, two irresistible attractions: a magnificent view of the Vieux Port, and a talented young chef who was a native of Marseille, and who therefore understood fish.

During the short walk down to the port, Reboul did his best to explain why buying a house in France was such a prolonged and exhausting process. "The French find it very difficult to trust anybody when it comes to business, particularly property transactions. I suppose one can't really blame them, because every old house has its history, and it's not unusual down here to find that one room, or an outside toilet, or a part of the garden, still belongs to a distant relative who might easily cause trouble. Obviously, this has to be foreseen, and dealt with legally. But perhaps just as important is the French love of bureaucracy. We may throw up our hands and complain about it, but in the end we accept it. I think we find it comforting. Anything simple and fast would be deeply suspicious."

Reboul led them along the Quai du Port until they came to an unmarked door, painted dark green and set back from the street, with a discreet intercom set into the wall next to it. "Here we are," said Reboul. "As you can see, the owners feel they can do without advertising — apart from the best kind, which is word of mouth. Most of the people who come here are regulars; in fact, it's more like a club." He pressed the buzzer, murmured his name, and the door clicked open.

A flight of steps led up to the narrow, light-filled restaurant. At one end was a visible kitchen, separated from the rest of the room by a wall of glass. The other walls were dedicated to the memory of Marseille's favorite writer and filmmaker, Marcel Pagnol. Giant black-and-white photographs of the great man and famous scenes from his films shared the space with posters: *Manon des Sources, Fanny, Jean de Florette, La Femme du Boulanger,* and half a dozen others.

"Let me guess the chef's name," said Elena. "Marcel?"

Reboul grinned and shook his head. "Actually, it's Serge. But Pagnol is his great hobby. Ah, here comes his lovely wife."

A young woman with a broad smile and a fan of menus made her way through the tables to greet them.

"Julie!" said Reboul.

"Francis!" said Julie.

Embraces, kisses, and compliments were followed by introductions, and then Julie took them across the room and out onto the terrace. There were no more than a dozen tables, each with the same magnificent view: the boats of the Vieux Port, the glittering water, and, on the crest of a hill in the distance, the bell tower and the golden statue of the Madonna and Child crowning Notre-Dame de la Garde, a magnificent basilica built in 1864 on the foundations of a sixteenth-century fort.

Reboul settled himself and raised the flute of Champagne that had magically appeared. "In all good restaurants," he said, "one of the best appetizers is anticipation. A glass of something chilled and delicious, a menu of temptations, delightful company — there is no better way to put your taste buds on the *qui vive*. What shall we have? The *tartare de coquilles Saint-Jacques*? The homemade *foie gras*? Or the chef's pride and joy, the *bouillabaisse maison*? Decisions, decisions. Take your time, my friends, take your time."

While Elena, Sam, and Reboul were making up their minds, Coco Dumas was making do with a club sandwich on the high-speed TGV train to Paris. She was going to see her father, Alex, who had set her up in business more than fifteen years earlier. A self-made man and proud of it, Alex Dumas had made a great deal of money from business activities — which he never discussed — that took him from Belgium to Paris, often via Africa. He doted on his daughter, and, having recognized the talent she showed during her early years in architecture, he had thought of a way she could usefully fit in with his own business plans. He had been more than satisfied with the results, but now he was ready to retire; not, however, before making sure his precious Coco was set up for life.

As late afternoon faded into evening, the two of them sat in the living room of Dumas *père*'s apartment in the Rue de Lille — decorated and furnished to perfection by Coco — and discussed some interesting possibilities. By the time they went across the street to Le Bistrot de Paris for dinner, an idea was forming. But the details, those all-important details, had to be worked out. Meanwhile, there were Coco's future plans to consider. When Papa retired, what would his daughter do? She was beginning to tire of clients, with their nagging and their indecisiveness and their reluctance to do exactly as they were told. She, too, was ready for a change. An apartment in New York, perhaps, with a place in the Bahamas to escape to during those brutal Manhattan winters. A fresh start. It was a prospect that Coco found immensely appealing.

With considerable reluctance, Elena boarded the flight that would take her to Paris and the connection to Los Angeles. She felt distinctly cheated. All she wanted to do was spend time with Sam exploring their new house. She had thoughts of picnic lunches on the terrace, with a glass or two of *rosé* in the evening to toast the sunset. But it was not to be. She opened her briefcase to go, once again, through the paperwork. And there, tucked into a side pocket, were a few notes she had drafted for her letter of resignation. Just looking through them made her feel better.

It was a somber Frank Knox who greeted her the following day. As she already knew, he had followed the prudent insurer's custom of splitting the risk among other insurance companies. But even so, he was going to be hit hard, and he wanted to be absolutely sure that Elena's visit hadn't turned up something that could be used to soften the blow. They spent several hours going over Elena's visit to the Castellaci house in Nice, room by room. They went yet again through the entire Castellaci file. They reviewed the precedent established in similar cases. But it was no good. Unless it could be proved beyond doubt that the owner of the stolen diamonds was also the thief, the claim was watertight.

Frank Knox sighed. "I guess that's it. Now we have to tell the other companies what they're going to have to fork out." He took a glass and a bottle of Scotch from his desk drawer. "I'm really sorry, but we're going to have to go through all this again for them."

The thought of dealing with a bunch of suspicious insurance agents stiffened Elena's resolve. "I'm sorry, too, Frank, but I've had it. When this is over, I'm quitting." She took the letter of resignation from her briefcase and slid it across the desk.

Knox looked at it, sighed once more, emptied his glass, and shook his head. "Can't say I blame you."

Elena's call woke Sam up. "I have good news and bad news," she said. "I have to stay in L.A. for another couple of days." She paused for a moment. "But the good news is I've quit."

"Sweetheart, that's great. How do you feel about it?"

"Well, you know — sad for Frank, but otherwise pretty good." She paused. "No, otherwise it feels fantastic."

"I can hear you smiling."

"Listen, while you're waiting for me to get back, why don't you take a look around the inside of the house to see what needs to be done? I'll expect a full report, okay?"

"Yes, ma'am."

Sam decided to enlist the help of Reboul, a man who had a thorough grounding in the joys of renovation, having spent three years licking Le Pharo into shape. He was almost as excited as Sam, and on the twenty-five-minute walk over to the house he offered some basic advice on dealing with the Provençal architect.

"First," he said, "establish a strict budget — never popular, but necessary. Next, get a firm completion date written into the contract. This is even less popular. Finally, and the least popular of all, there should be penalty clauses if the work isn't done on time. Oh, and watch out for *les petits inconnus.*"

Sam laughed. "I would if I knew what they were."

"The little unknowns. They are every architect's best excuse — the unpredictable problems that delay the progress of the work and increase the price. This can be anything from a fractured sewage pipe to a colony of killer hornets in the roof. But — *quelle surprise!* — how were we to know?"

Reboul carried on with his litany of tips and warnings until the two men had walked up the narrow, stony drive and stopped in front of the house. "My friend, don't take anything I've said too seriously. This is a very special property."

And no doubt it would be, but at the moment generous doses of optimism and imagination were required. There were windows, but they did their best to ignore the view, and they were small. So too were the rooms, with a tiny kitchen barely big enough to swing a saucepan, and a somber living room. Upstairs, one garret led to another — five in all — and the single bathroom, with a strong whiff of damp and a drip-stained bathtub, actively discouraged any thoughts of hygiene.

But once outside, everything changed. The terrace, although in need of repair, went around three sides of the house, giving the choice of sun or shade all through the day. And the view, in every direction, was incredible. It was this view, Sam and Reboul agreed, that had to be brought into the house, with much bigger windows and fewer, but larger and lighter, rooms. "Gut it," was Reboul's advice, "and make it selfish — just for the two of you."

This raised the question of who should do the gutting. Preferably someone local, who had contacts with the most reliable workmen; someone with taste; and, if possible, someone who was fluent in English. Reboul's mind went back to Tommy Van Buren's house outside Cannes, and Coco Dumas.

"She would be ideal for this job," said Reboul. "But as you know, Sam, I have a problem with her. Let's find a few other architects, and see what you think of them."

"What about the guy who did Le Pharo for you? He did a terrific job."

"He did. And he sent me some terrific bills." Reboul winced at the memory. "In fact, he retired to Martinique on the proceeds."

CHAPTER 6

Sam stood waiting for Elena in the arrivals area at the Marseille airport, playing the game of Spot the Parisian. Although not yet full summer, the vacation season was off to an early start, and refugees from the north were becoming more and more numerous. They could often be identified by what they were wearing: the pessimists still in scarves and heavy jackets, the optimists dressed ready for a day at the beach. It occurred to Sam that this was the first time he had waited at the airport as a homeowner, and therefore almost a native; he did his best to look like a Marseillais.

He was expecting to meet a weary, travel-wrinkled Elena, and was delighted to see instead a fresh-faced, smiling vision coming toward him. As she explained on the way to the car, Frank Knox had been so grateful to her for staying on to help out that he had bumped her up to first class for the flight back.

"I had a full-length bed," she said, "a couple of glasses of Champagne, and ten hours sleep. Heaven. Even better, when I woke up I remembered that I'd quit." Her face was one huge beam.

"You're not going to miss it?"

"Are you kidding? Does anyone miss toothache? Anyway, I won't have time to miss it — I've got a house to fix up."

The house was the main topic of conversation on the drive back to Le Pharo. Elena cross-examined Sam about the state of everything — windows, floors, plumbing, roof — until Sam suggested that these were delicate matters best left to an architect.

"Any ideas?" asked Elena.

"Francis has been working on it. He's asking some of his friends if they can recommend anyone. This is all pretty new to me. I haven't had too much experience with architects. Have you?"

"Once, when I moved into my apartment in L.A. But it didn't work out."

"No?"

"Let's say we weren't aesthetically compatible. That's how I put it when I fired him."

They arrived at Le Pharo, dropped off

Elena's suitcase, and went downstairs in search of Reboul. They found him on the terrace, having a drink with Hervé, the police report of the Castellaci robbery on the table between them.

"Ah, here she is, my favorite insurance executive. Welcome back." Reboul stood up to present Elena and Sam to Hervé. "We've been looking at the report you left." He poured glasses of *rosé* for them before sitting down. "I'm sorry to say that it doesn't look very hopeful. I'll let Hervé explain."

Hervé, normally a jovial man, looked unusually serious. "It seems to me that my colleagues in Nice have produced a very professional report. All the relevant details are there, and I'm afraid I have to agree with their conclusion that there is little hope of recovering the diamonds or finding the thief." He paused for a sip of wine. "Robberies like this are, fortunately, very rare. I can think of only one or two in the past five years or so — there was one in Monaco, another about eighteen months ago in Antibes, and now this. In and out, no signs of forced entry, no prints, nothing." He shook his head. "And no publicity, either. Robberies like this are not glamorous or dramatic, like the jobs that are done in Cannes with guns and getaways on Harley-Davidson motorcycles. There's no story. Nobody cares — it's just rich people having some bad luck, that's all."

Sam was frowning. "Did the guys in Nice check on maids, cooks, chauffeurs, people like that, who are in and out of the house all the time?"

Hervé sighed. "Of course. In this case, the staff were given the night off, and they all had alibis." He tapped the folder in front of him. "The details are in here. As I said, a very professional report."

"So what happens now? Does this just get filed and forgotten?"

"Sam, if you think you can find something that a team of highly trained specialists overlooked, good luck to you. My personal theory — not to be repeated — is that Castellaci arranged for the jewels to be stolen so that he could pick up the insurance." He saw Elena wince. "Sorry, my dear. But experience has shown me that the rich can be quite astonishingly dishonest." He glanced at his watch and stood up. "I must go." He looked at Sam, and winked. "I feel the urge to arrest somebody."

Early the following morning, Elena dragged Sam out of bed and thrust him, still protesting, into the shower. She hadn't yet had time to inspect the inside of their house, and could hardly wait to be done with breakfast. This was to be a big day. Reboul's friends had recommended some architects, and interviews had been arranged. These would take place on site, and Elena was almost pawing the ground with anticipation.

On their way over to the house, Sam passed on the advice that Reboul had given him. "Fixed budget. Firm delivery date. And penalty clauses. OK?"

"How about aesthetic compatibility?"

"That too."

When they arrived, Elena immediately went inside, leaving Sam to pace around the house and work out where and when the sun would hit. They had decided to create a breakfast terrace to catch the morning sun, a lunchtime terrace in the shade, and an evening terrace for drinks and a view of the sunset. Reboul had warned Sam not to rely on umbrellas for shade because, as he said, when the Mistral is blowing it can take an umbrella halfway to Corsica. So shadows cast by the house and trees would have to provide the necessary patches of shade.

Sam was making some rough notes on his iPad when Elena emerged, skipped across to him, and put her arms round his neck.

"It's going to be great. Francis was right — gut it and start over. But tell me something: How can you have five bedrooms with one lousy little bathroom? Is that an old French tradition?"

Sam was stopped from speculating on the bathroom habits of the French by the arrival, in a Porsche convertible, of the first architect. According to the names and times on Sam's list, this was Christian de Beaufort.

He was a most elegant gentleman, with a mane of silver hair, beautifully turned out in a black linen suit. He was accompanied by an equally chic young woman carrying a briefcase, who was having some difficulty negotiating the uneven stony ground in her perilously high heels. After introductions had been made and the view admired, de Beaufort insisted that he and his assistant should be left to look around the house on their own, without any distractions. Twenty minutes passed.

When de Beaufort came out, brushing dust off his jacket, it quickly became clear that he had not been impressed by what he had seen. "Of course," he said, "with this property, the view is everything; the house is secondary. Above all, it needs to be substantially enlarged. At the moment, for instance, there is nowhere for the servants to sleep. Naturally, everything is possible, but," and here he shrugged, "I don't think that I am the man for the job. My work is on a larger scale. *Désolé.*" And with that, he put on his sunglasses and he and his assistant inserted themselves into the Porsche.

Sam was pleased to see that Elena was laughing. "The nerve of the guy," she said, "although he had a point. Where *will* we put the servants?"

De Beaufort's lukewarm assessment of the house was a taste of things to come. As the day wore on, three more architects came and went. One suggested razing the house to the ground and replacing it with a modern glass cube. Another wanted to add a penthouse and turn the ground floor into an indoor swimming pool. A third was practically speechless with shock when Sam mentioned budgets and penalty clauses. "How do you expect an artist to work like that?" he said, as he flounced off. By late afternoon, Elena and Sam had to face the fact that they hadn't made much progress.

Over a drink with Reboul that evening, Elena confessed that she had been disappointed that all the candidates — and indeed the vast majority of architects — were men.

"Why aren't there more women?" She looked accusingly at Sam, as though it were his fault, but gave him no chance to reply before climbing on to her hobby horse. "Women understand kitchens; most men don't. Women realize that even the closest couples need some personal space. Women do bathrooms much better. Women aren't afraid of working to budgets. Women appreciate the importance of well-organized storage space. In other words, they're much, much more practical. And another thing," she said, "they don't let their egos get in the way of their work."

While Reboul was listening to this, he couldn't help remembering a few architectural hiccups that had occurred while Le Pharo was being renovated — mistakes that would not have been made by a woman: a lack of full-length closet space and a shower like a huge deep-freeze, in particular. He sighed as he came to the obvious conclusion.

"I remember you liked what Coco Dumas had done to Tommy Van Buren's house. Would you think of using her?"

Elena put her hand out and squeezed Reboul's arm. "Not in a million years, if it would be a problem for you."

"I can always duck. But seriously, she's

very professional, there wouldn't be any language difficulties, and, of course, she's the acceptable sex. All I ask is that you keep her well away from Le Pharo."

Elena leaned over and kissed Reboul on the cheek. "It's a deal."

Sam was by now getting used to Elena's determination not to be outdressed by French women. Banned from the bedroom, he had settled into the sitting room next door to wait for her to appear. They were going to Nice for a meeting with Coco Dumas in her office, and, as Elena had explained more than once, her appearance would send a strong signal. French women take these things seriously; they are quite open about inspecting another woman's outfit, and, if it passes scrutiny, she is more likely to be treated as an equal, worthy of respect.

"Well, what do you think?" Elena stood framed in the bedroom doorway, wearing a simple silk dress the color of pale lavender that set off her black hair and lightly tanned complexion.

"Lovely," said Sam. "You look good enough to eat. She'll be insanely jealous."

"Perfect. Let's go."

The drive from Marseille to Nice is an

easy run on the *autoroute,* and they arrived at the Negresco with half an hour to spare before the appointment, plenty of time to take in the sea air along the Promenade des Anglais, an elegant thoroughfare built in 1830 with English money. Its original purpose was to provide refined young English ladies with somewhere to stroll where they wouldn't be pestered by "licentious locals."

Sam passed this historical nugget on to Elena, who was immediately intrigued by the thought of licentious locals. "What about that guy?" she said, as a young man with a baseball cap worn backwards hurtled past them on a skateboard. "Do you think he's licentious? How can a girl tell?"

They stopped for a quick coffee, and Elena showed Sam a laconic text message from Frank Knox that had come in overnight: *Please tell Castellacis they will be paid in full. Ouch.* It was a reminder that the mysterious theft remained a mystery.

"Poor Frank," said Elena. "I bet he can't wait to retire."

"What's he going to do?"

"Same as me, I guess — relax, and forget about the insurance business."

"You're doing pretty well so far. Tell me — you've met the famous Coco. What did you think of her?"

"Tough. Smart. I can imagine her being quite a handful. But what I've seen of her work is terrific. What are you laughing at?"

"You've just described yourself. The two of you will make quite a pair. This is going to be fun. Oh, I meant to ask you: Is there going to be a problem between you two after that little misunderstanding at the party?"

"With Francis, you mean? No, not at all. When I called her to make a date for the meeting, I explained, and she was fine. Actually, she said she can't wait to meet you."

CHAPTER 7

Coco met them at the door of her suite —
smiling, charming, and, as expected, quite
unabashed about her detailed inspection of
Elena's outfit. Sam was amused to see Elena
doing exactly the same thing, her eyes going
from the summer sandals that displayed Coco's scarlet toenails, up past the beige linen
trousers and on to a sleeveless top of black
silk. With this vital exchange completed,
Coco led them to her office.

It was simple, uncluttered, verging on
minimalist — a complete contrast to the
Belle Époque splendors of the rest of the
hotel. A collection of austere black-and-
white architectural photographs hung on
walls the color of pale cream. In the center
of the room was a round black conference
table, with half a dozen black leather chairs.
The floor was dark polished wood, and in
one corner stood a small bronze statue of
Mies van der Rohe, on a plinth engraved

with his inscrutable but famous motto: *Less Is More.* The overall effect of the room, as Sam said later, had made him feel that he should have worn his best black suit for the occasion.

While they were getting settled around the table, Coco gave them a brief description of the premises. "Through that door over there, I have a small apartment — nothing very grand, but it's convenient. And through the door opposite are two offices; one for me, and one for my colleague, Monsieur Gregoire."

Right on cue, Gregoire appeared, welcomed Elena and Sam with crushing handshakes, flexed his shoulders as though preparing for a bruising physical encounter, and launched into his mantra of no bribes, no kickbacks. Despite the fact that he had gone through this dozens of times, he still managed to sound mildly astonished that, in a wicked world, such scrupulous probity still existed. He ended with a brief outline of the Cabinet Dumas's terms of business before handing over to Coco.

The leather albums were produced, and Coco took Elena and Sam through a guided tour of her work, stopping from time to time to respond to questions and comments. "And now," she said to Elena with a smile, "it's your turn. I want to hear all about your new house."

Elena produced her iPad and moved closer to Coco so that they could share the screen. "The place is a mess right now, but it could be great. Anyway, here's the 'before' part of the project." And she began to show Coco the photographs, starting with the interior of the house: the dreadful bathroom, the poky bedrooms, the funereal living room, the impossible kitchen. Sam was relieved to see that the two women seemed to be getting on, exchanging comments and even laughing at the architectural horror story as it unfolded. But when she saw photographs of the view, Coco was immediately enthusiastic. "Now I understand," she said. "You fell in love with the view. Who wouldn't?"

From there, Coco started to make all the right noises about gutting the interior and bringing the view into the house, and Sam could see Elena becoming more and more enthusiastic. Perhaps it was time, he thought, to put the brakes on.

"Just one thing," he said, "before you bring in the bulldozer. We have terms of business too." He went through his short list of strict budget, firm completion date, and penalty clauses. To Sam's surprise,

Coco was nodding at everything she heard. "That's fine with us," she said. "That's the way we work." And on this cordial note, all that remained was to agree on a date for Coco to meet them the following week at the property, and to ask if she could recommend somewhere for lunch, which she was happy to do: Le Club de la Promenade, two minutes from the Negresco.

The restaurant was decorated, as all beach restaurants seem to be, in a maritime color scheme of blue and white, with the occasional fishing net draped in a picturesque position. The owner, a deeply tanned woman of a certain age, wearing a white T-shirt and hot pants, detached herself from the bar and came over to guide them to a table. *"Voilà,"* she said with a smile, "I give you a table with a sea view." And there indeed was a glimpse of the sea, just visible between the clumps of beach umbrellas and the rows of bodies — every color from medium rare to well done — that were lined up cheek by oiled jowl. A waitress, dressed like all her colleagues in white T-shirt and hot pants, put two menus on the table and suggested that an *apéritif* might help them make their choice.

The postmortem began even before the first glass of *rosé.* They agreed that it had been a most encouraging morning. Sam admitted that he hadn't been at all sure that Coco and Elena would get on after their first rather edgy meeting at the Van Buren house.

"I told you," said Elena. "I straightened that out when I called her. Anyway, when she met you, she calmed down."

"I have that effect on women," said Sam. "But then you seemed to get on pretty well. How do you feel about working with her?"

"Fine. I like what she's done for her other clients: simple, good taste. I get the feeling that her houses work."

"Are you sure we can trust her not to bother Francis?"

"I already told you," said Elena. "I'll make sure she behaves." Sam had no doubt that she would.

Their lunch of fresh fish, crisp and perfectly cooked French fries, and *fiadone,* a Corsican-style cheesecake, was all the more enjoyable because they were going through the first and most pleasant stage of property renovation. The ideas were coming thick and fast, the bills hadn't started to arrive, the expensive and unforeseen problems, *les petits inconnus,* hadn't yet surfaced — it was all very exciting. Even Sam, a man not normally given to excessive enthusiasms, found himself mentally moving in to a house of sun-kissed perfection.

Meanwhile, Coco and her colleague were also having a post-mortem, and Monsieur Gregoire, no longer the mild-mannered second fiddle, had become Coco's equal, assertive and opinionated. And he was not at all in favor of taking on Elena and Sam's house.

"Our business," he said, "has been built on big, multimillion-euro projects, owned by seriously rich people. This little shack is just a distraction." He stood up, and walked over to the window, shaking his head. "A waste of your time."

Coco sighed. There were times when she found Gregoire's obsession with money intensely irritating. "I'm getting a little tired of rich people and their vast mansions. This could be fantastic," she said. "I like the owners, and it would amuse me. I'm going to do it."

"A waste of your time," he said again. "You seem to have forgotten why our business has been so successful."

"And you seem to have forgotten the name of the business: It's Cabinet Dumas. Not Cabinet Gregoire. I'm going to do it."

Coco's words stayed with Gregoire as he made his way along the Promenade des Anglais, and they rankled. More and more often in recent weeks, he felt that she was treating him as though he were nothing more than her secretary. In fact, during the several years they had worked together, he knew he had made substantial and profitable contributions to the business. But he was still an employee, and not an equal partner. Promises had been hinted at, but never followed up. Gregoire had run out of patience and money. His gambling hadn't been going well. He needed a big hit.

His mood brightened as he reached the beach restaurant where he was meeting a promising new girlfriend for lunch. Le Poisson Nu — the Naked Fish — was a simple place that served good, simple food. But what attracted regular clients of both sexes was the relaxed dress code, which decreed that a swimsuit, however brief, was all one needed to wear for lunch.

Gregoire went into the primitive dressing room to change before picking his way through the forest of tanned flesh that was standing at the bar and sitting at the tables. The promising girlfriend was already at their table, looking even more promising. On the two previous occasions they had met, she had been fully dressed. Today, all that saved her from nudity were a few artfully placed scraps of bikini. Gregoire sucked in his stomach and went to join her.

Far away, on the other side of the Atlantic, Kathy and Conor Fitzgerald were preparing for another grueling day of fulfilling their social obligations. These were their last few days in New York before leaving to go to Paris and then down to their house on Cap Ferrat for the summer, and the giddy round of farewell lunches, soirées, and dinners was in full swing.

Fitzgerald, now approaching sixty, was reputed to be the richest grocer in America. Starting forty years earlier with a small convenience store in his hometown of Boston, he had since accumulated two major supermarket chains, apartment buildings in Miami and Los Angeles, a string of racehorses, a duplex on Central Park South, the house on Cap Ferrat, and a number of wives, of whom Kathy was the youngest, blondest, and most recent. She matched his ability to make money with a talent for spending it — furs, jewels, couture clothes, she loved them all, and her doting husband was happy to indulge her.

Over breakfast, the Fitzgeralds were going over their social plans for France. Kathy was anxious to meet what she called a younger crowd, as a change from their older New York friends.

Fitzgerald leaned across the breakfast table and patted her cheek. "No problem, honey. We'll throw a party once we've settled in. Why don't you talk to that gal who fixed up the house? She must know just about everyone down there. She can round up a few locals for you."

"Fitz, you're a doll. And you're sure it's OK about my fitness trainer?"

"Absolutely. There's plenty of room on the plane. Just as long as she doesn't want me to start doing push-ups."

Kathy was delighted at the thought of getting in touch once again with Coco Dumas, whom she had met during the renovation of the house on Cap Ferrat. Kathy had been impressed by Coco's chic and her ideas; Coco had been pleasantly surprised to find a woman who, unlike so many of her clients, had managed to remain relatively normal despite her rich, pampered life. A mutual liking had developed. And so, when they spoke later that day, the first few minutes had been devoted to verbal air kisses and the exchange of social news before Kathy broached the subject of the party.

"I'd love it if you could help me out. We've decided to give a party at the house. We'll have our house guests, of course, but they're all old friends from New York, and I'd like to invite some fresh faces — you know, some fun locals: young, amusing, and English-speaking would be perfect. What do you think?"

Coco didn't need to think for too long. At that time of year, the Riviera was crawling with people who needed to be entertained every evening, ideally by going to smart parties in fashionable houses. "That won't be a problem," she said. "I'll get back to you with a few suggestions."

She left her office, poured herself a glass of wine, and went out to the terrace. It was early evening, the sun was low on the horizon, and the day's appointments and phone calls were over. It was an ideal time to think.

Her mind went back to her exchange earlier in the day with Gregoire. It was true that he had brought in several good clients over the years, and he took care of the financial side of the business efficiently enough. But lately he had become increasingly argumentative and tiresome, more like a difficult client than a partner. Coco sighed. She was more than ready for a new life in New York.

She was distracted by the sound of a chair

scraping the floor in her office. She had left the door open, and when she went through it, she found Gregoire hunched over one of the leather-bound books that she used in her presentations. She decided to forget about their exchange earlier in the day, and sat down next to him with a smile.

"Well, Greg. Doing some homework?"

"Oh — just catching up on some of our past triumphs."

"What have you got there?"

"The Fitzgerald house. They're coming over soon, aren't they?"

"Yes. They'll be here all summer."

Gregoire was shaking his head as he closed the book. "How the rich live. God, it must be great."

Coco had known Gregoire long enough to be wary whenever he started to make remarks about money. They inevitably led to discussions about his salary, his hope of becoming a full partner, his desperate need of a new car, and other sensitive and expensive subjects.

She was looking at her watch as she stood up. "I'm going to be late. See you in the morning."

CHAPTER 8

Elena was smiling as she came out of the kitchen and went over to the breakfast table, where Sam was brooding over his first coffee of the day.

"OK, it's all set," she said. "We're going shopping this morning."

"Lucky us," said Sam, whose enthusiasm for shopping with Elena, never great, had almost entirely disappeared after several grueling days going through Marseille's furniture showrooms and fabric stores. "And what are we buying today?"

"Food. Don't you remember? Alphonse offered to take us to one of his favorite places, and today's the day. Isn't that great?"

Sam brightened up. Shopping he could eat was the kind of shopping he liked. He finished his coffee and stood up, allowing Elena to smooth away the croissant crumbs that had fallen on his chest. "Why is it I never get to do that to you?" he said.

Elena was saved from answering by the arrival of Alphonse, dapper and dressed for shopping in a blue-and-white striped shirt worn over white pants, the ensemble finished off by navy-blue espadrilles and a Louis Vuitton baseball cap. He was carrying a large white canvas shopping bag in each hand. He gave one to Sam and the other to Elena, explaining that he needed both hands free for haggling.

"Today," he said, "we shall concentrate on fruit, vegetables, and cheese. Meat needs an entire morning to itself; so does fish. We must do those another time. Olivier is driving us today to Saint-Florian, a village with an excellent market where all the local producers have stands — everything from asparagus to zucchini. *Allez!*"

On their way to Saint-Florian, Alphonse went through his shopping list.

"I need asparagus, if we're not too late; melons and peaches; some Rattes, the connoisseur's potato; zucchini flowers, olives, and, of course, garlic and basil. Not to forget my favorite goat cheese. After that, I am the slave of inspiration. If I should see some perfectly ripe avocados, figs in their prime, or some broad beans worthy of my warm bean-and-bacon salad, then we must have those too. I always say that one should keep an open mind with an open mouth."

Like so many villages in Provence, Saint-Florian had been built on a hill, with the oldest buildings on top, where they hoped to be safe from attack by rapacious neighbors. Over the centuries, more peaceful times had encouraged building on the lower slopes of the hill, and eventually the construction of a large parking area. This was taken over for a day each week, when market stalls replaced cars and games of *boules.*

There must have been fifty or sixty of these stalls, selling fruits, vegetables, eggs, herbs, cheeses, and a few nonedible items, principally flowers and ladies' underwear. Led by Alphonse, the three of them shuffled through the crowd until they came to one of the larger stands, overflowing with vegetables and presided over by a burly, gray-haired man with a seamed, brown face that lit up at the sight of them. He came out from behind his lettuce display and embraced Alphonse, kissing him loudly on each cheek.

"Eh, *vieux con*! Where have you been hiding? And who are these two? Your children? *Les pauvres.*"

Introductions were made, with Regis the stallholder taking the opportunity to admire

Elena's bosom as he bent over to kiss her hand. He eventually stood up, released her hand, and sighed. "*Adorable.* And now, what can I do for you?"

Regis listened as Alphonse went through his list. "*Bon.* Most of these I have. But for melons and peaches, you must go to Elodie; and for the goat cheese, of course, there is nobody but Benjamin. Now then — come around to the back of the stall, where, as you know, I keep my treasures."

He led them to the back of the stall, which was a miniature version of the front, but with different produce. Here, instead of lettuces and leeks, carrots and cauliflowers and cabbages, Regis had arranged his more special items: zucchini flowers, asparagus, the noble Ratte potatoes, shining green and black olives, all arranged like jewels on their wooden trays.

"Since the asparagus season is over here, I have made a new friend across the Channel in England, where the season conveniently finishes later than it does here," said Regis. "And he sent me these. Not Provençal, of course, but not bad. Not bad at all." He pointed at a tray of asparagus, then picked one out. "You see? A good, bright green color. The tips are closed, as they should be. The spear is straight, and firm to the touch. And, most important, if you try to bend it, it should crack. *Tenez.*" He passed the spear to Elena. "Go ahead."

Elena took the spear, holding it in front of her with both hands, and applied pressure. The spear snapped with an audible crack. *"Bravo,"* said Regis, and looked enquiringly at Alphonse, who ordered half a dozen *bottes.* These were passed to Sam, with instructions to store the bunches carefully in his bag.

It was the same ritual with the zucchini flowers, the potatoes, and the olives. Regis would present an example of each to Elena, pointing out its readiness for the table, its superb color and texture — in short, its flawless perfection — before taking Alphonse's order.

And then the discussion about payment began. Regis mentioned a price. Alphonse feigned shock, shaking one hand as though his fingers had been burned and throwing his arms in the air before turning out the pockets on each side of his trousers, empty except for a few cents. Regis shook his head, sucked his teeth, reconsidered with a great show of reluctance, and lowered the price fractionally. Alphonse, his reputation as a keen haggler intact, nodded his approval and produced a well-stuffed wallet from his back pocket.

Elena and Sam had been watching the performance with interest. "Do you think you could do that?" asked Sam. "You know, haggling?"

Elena shook her head. "I tried it once. Didn't work."

"Where was this?"

"Dallas. Nieman Marcus."

Alphonse and Regis, the best of friends once more, embraced and exchanged fond insults before Alphonse, with a lordly wave of the hand to Sam, by now carrying both shopping bags, set off for Elodie, her melons, and her peaches.

They found her, as Alphonse had warned them, bursting with indignation. She was a slight, pretty woman, with a tanned face and blonde hair pulled back in a ponytail, and she barely had time for a double kiss with Alphonse and a nod toward Elena and Sam before she launched into her least favorite topic: those dastardly Spanish peach growers.

"Do you know," she said, poking Alphonse in the chest with an agitated finger, "they've worked out this new *arnaque,* their latest scam. They deliver to supermarkets in France without first setting a price; they see what the French price is, then they undercut

it. How can we compete? French produc-/
tion of peaches has halved in the past ten
years. *C'est scandaleux!*"

Alphonse, who had heard similar com-
plaints before, patted her on the shoulder.
"I know, I know. But what you must remember, *chérie,* is that your peaches have a
flavor, a finesse, that no Spanish peach can
hope to equal." He turned to Elena and
Sam. "Look at these peaches! These are very
early — encouraged, no doubt, in Elodie's
hothouse — and they are superb. If only
Monet were here to paint them. We must
have the whole tray." He picked out a peach
and held it up. "The secrets of choosing a
ripe peach are color, feel, and smell." He
passed the peach to Elena. "You see? There
is a uniform rosiness, with no green patches.
Now squeeze it: firm, not mushy. And smell
it, as you would a glass of fine wine."

Elena inhaled. "Wonderful. A vintage
peach."

By now, Elodie had regained her good
humor, and was ready to move on to her
melons — her Cavaillon melons — which
she said even a Spaniard would have to
admit were the finest in the world. She
handed one over to Alphonse, who weighed
it thoughtfully in his hand and tapped it
with his knuckles. "Did you hear that?" he

said to Elena. "That is the correct sound, as if the melon were hollow. Now we must see if it's ripe." He passed the melon to Elena. "At the top, you see what we call — excuse me — the nipple. At the bottom there is a little stalk. This is the *pécou,* or tail, and it should be the same color as the melon. Now look closely. If there is a tiny crack around the tail, tinged with red, that is a sure sign of ripeness. We call it 'the drop of blood.' In fact, it's formed by sugar coming from inside the melon and crystallizing."

The melons and peaches were paid for and packed. Elena and Alphonse strode off in search of cheese, and a heavily laden Sam followed behind. After a brief stop for basil and garlic, they arrived at the stall of Benjamin, a good-looking young man with a beard. "Don't be put off by his youth," said Alphonse. "He grew up with goats. He was making cheese while he was still at school." He turned to Benjamin. "*Alors, jeune homme.* What do you recommend today?"

Benjamin grinned, his teeth white against his black beard, and pointed to the display on his stall. "They are all good, but there is one cheese here that every man should taste before he dies: my Brousse du Rove."

"Ah," said Alphonse. "I had hoped it would be here. We are very fortunate. This is goat cheese at its best. See how white it is? See how creamy it is? This is a cheese that is just as happily eaten with a touch of black olive *tapenade* as with a fresh fig. In other words, you can have it as an appetizer or at the end of the meal as a dessert. Or both." He took a teaspoon from a dish on the stand and offered a spoonful to Elena.

At first, there was no reaction. Then she began to nod. "Oh boy," she said. "Oh boy." Alphonse beamed. Benjamin beamed. Sam started to make extra room in one of his bags.

They had one last stop to make. Alphonse wanted them to see a local curiosity, which he described to them as a *bar roulant,* or mobile bar, perhaps the only one in Provence. "Another example," he said, "of French ingenuity."

They found it at the entrance to the market — a large white van marked on one side with a sign that read *Réserves Médicales,* or Medical Supplies, because, as Alphonse said, a traveling bar was "not exactly legal." On the van's other side, a panel had been dropped down to make a counter, now decorated with several customers in various stages of thirst. Prominently displayed was an easel with a small blackboard, on which was written:

LISTE DES VINS
Rouge 3 Euros
Rosé 2 Euros
Rosé Supérieur 4 Euros

The two proprietors, so Alphonse told them, were a husband-and-wife team, Jacky and Flo. Flo was responsible for driving; Jacky was in charge of everything liquid, a responsibility which, if his almost luminous nose was anything to go by, he took very seriously.

"I'm buying," said Sam. "Money's no object. *Rosé Supérieur* all around."

It arrived in small tumblers of thick glass, and tasted surprisingly good.

"A toast," said Elena, "To dear Alphonse, who will make me a kitchen diva one of these days. Thanks so much for this morning."

"A pleasure, my dear. Do you have any questions?"

Sam raised a hand. "What's for lunch?"

CHAPTER 9

"Hear that? It's the sound of summer." Sam and Elena had just arrived at their house. It was barely 8:00 a.m. but the builders were already there. "The drowsy hum of the cement mixer, the chirping of the jackhammer — makes you glad we got here so early, doesn't it?"

Elena winced at the thud of falling masonry. "Is this a normal time for them to start work?"

"Francis told me they like to do the heavy stuff before it gets too hot. Later on, during high summer, the temperatures will be up in the nineties by midday, and that's a little warm for swinging a pickaxe."

Although it had been only a few days since the start of work, it looked as though a surprising amount of progress had been made. All the windows and exterior doors were gone, the openings were being enlarged, and flagstones were stacked and ready to be put in place on the terraces around the house. The dingy bathtub had been uprooted and left, brimming with rubble, next to the truck that would take it away. For Elena, all this noise and activity was an exciting change after years of living in ready-made apartments in L.A. She was busy taking photographs when Coco appeared in the doorway. "Hold it right there," Elena said, aiming her camera. "Look as if you're having fun." Coco smiled obligingly, and came out to join them. Sam noticed that she and Elena were now on kissing terms; he had to make do with a handshake.

Even dressed for dust and destruction, Coco managed to look crisp and stylish in white overalls, with a gauzy turquoise scarf at her throat. "Some good news," she said. "The roof is in much better shape than the rest of the house, so we're looking at a few repairs, and not a total replacement. That's going to save a lot of time. And the good news for you, Monsieur Budget," she added, looking at Sam, "is that we'll also save some money."

Sam nodded his approval. "Great. Now we can have the gold bathroom taps and his-and-hers Jacuzzis." He looked at Coco's raised eyebrows. "Just kidding."

The good news continued. All the partition walls would be demolished by the end of the week, and the scruffy floor tiles removed. Within two weeks, Coco promised, the new construction could begin. And so, by the time Elena and Sam left the site at the end of the morning, they were in the highest of spirits.

To add to the pleasures of the day, they were meeting Philippe, their journalist friend, for lunch. He had called to say he had something to celebrate, and had asked them to meet him in his favorite haunt, Le Bistrot d'Edouard, a restaurant dedicated to *tapas* in all their delightful variety.

On their way into Marseille, Elena was trying to predict the cause of the celebration. "He's finally going to marry Mimi," she said, "or he's been made editor of the paper. Or he's got a book contract."

"What makes you say that?"

"That's what journalists do. They see all these stories coming into the newsroom. A lot of them, the juicy ones, are impossible to use in the paper for legal reasons — and they see a best seller. Keep the story, change the names, and call it fiction. Simple."

Sam remained silent, digesting this literary revelation while he concentrated on his maneuvers with the tangled traffic. By the time he'd found a parking spot and beaten off an indignant challenge from a Renault with its blaring horn in overdrive, he was ready for a drink.

They found Philippe at a table on the terrace of the restaurant, an ice bucket already loaded. He stood up, spreading his arms in welcome before hugging them both. With his fashionably distressed jeans, black shirt, sunglasses, three-day stubble, and white jacket, he could have been taken for a hip refugee from the Cannes Film Festival.

Sam fingered the lapel of the white jacket. "This is all pretty dapper, Philippe. What happened to the suit?"

"I've changed my look," said Philippe. "It's a career move." He filled their glasses, and raised his own. "Let's drink to my new job." In between *pata negra* ham, artichokes of the palest violet with parmesan, and an extended procession of *tapas,* Philippe brought them up to date.

He had left the local newspaper to work for *Salut!,* a magazine covering the antics and social life of celebrity France, and his assigned beat was Provence and the Riviera. "From Marseille to Monaco," Philippe said, "I shall hunt down *les people,* the rich and famous, and bring their news to all our readers. The magazine has given me a car, so I can get rid of the scooter, and the expenses are" — he paused to kiss his fingertips — "prodigious. Last week I was in Saint-Paul de Vence for the spring exhibition at the Fondation Maeght, tomorrow there's a twenty-first-birthday party here in Marseille for one of the Cartier girls, and next week I'm off to Menton for a wedding. Oh, I almost forgot — if I come up with ideas for special events, there's a budget for them as well. How about that?" He sat back in his chair, the picture of a man who has just achieved a dream.

Elena was smiling at his enthusiasm as she offered her congratulations. "Just one thing," she said. "What does Mimi think about all this gallivanting around?"

Philippe leaned forward, tapping his nose with an index finger. "She's my photographer, so she comes with me. Not bad, eh?"

Lunch almost drifted into dinner as the three of them discussed possible projects for Philippe: a visit with the minister of tourism at the Fort de Brégançon, the president's old summer vacation retreat; a piece on members of the floating summer population and their three-hundred-foot yachts; topless waterskiing in Saint-Tropez; an evening at the Casino of Monte Carlo; a *Salut!* celebrity fashion show in the Palais des Festivals in Cannes; Philippe was furiously making notes.

"What you have to remember," he said, "are two things. First, people get bored with lying on the beach, and so by the evening they're ready for anything that moves. And second, they all love seeing their photographs in a glossy magazine. It makes them feel like stars." He shrugged. "So I have human nature working for me."

"Philippe's right," said Sam, as they were driving back to Le Pharo. "People's obsession with celebrity is amazing. They want to read about it and they want to rub shoulders with it, which makes them feel that they're part of it. Weird."

"Thanks, professor. So being famous has never appealed to you?"

"I haven't met many celebrities, but the ones I have met were so pleased with themselves it kind of put me off the whole idea. I'm happy to be anonymous, and to have the love of an adorable woman."

"Sam, you are so full of it." He could almost hear her rolling her eyes.

Back at Le Pharo, they took to the pool and swam off the aftereffects of lunch; and after ten lengths, all those *tapas* were no more than a pleasant memory. Drying off by the side of the pool, Sam looked up at the clean blue sky and gave a sigh of contentment.

"I can tell," said Elena. "You're lying there missing L.A."

"Sure. Five million cars, smog, what's not to miss?"

"Do you think we could live here full-time?"

"Do you?"

Before Elena could answer, they heard a whistle coming from the terrace behind them. It was Reboul, and he was holding up what looked very much like a bottle of *rosé*. They pulled on terrycloth robes and went over to join him.

He was still in his business suit, looking a little tired. He'd spent the morning with his bankers, and the afternoon at a meeting with the suppliers of equipment for a development project just outside Marseille that he was funding. The meeting had dragged on, and had not gone well. "God knows I've lived here long enough to know by now," he said, "that everything you want done down here should be done between October and April. This year, there are three national holidays in May, all of them on a Thursday. Naturally, everyone takes those Fridays off to make a nice long weekend. So that's six working days lost in that one month. Now here we are in June, and already they're slowing down, rehearsing for July and August, when nothing gets done. Factories close, and we'll be lucky if orders we're placing now are delivered by the middle of September." He shook his head. "And they never stop moaning about how bad the French economy is." He poured the wine and raised his glass. "So I hope you had a better day than I had."

"Poor Francis," said Elena. "I hate to tell you, but we had a great day. It's all happening so fast."

"Try not to get too excited. Destruction is always faster than construction. Tell me — how do you like working with Coco?"

As both Sam and Elena said, first impressions were very good. Elena had been particularly impressed by Coco's attention to detail, and her grasp of boring but important matters like the correct placement of a new septic tank and the most efficient distribution of the alarm sensors. Less boring but equally important was the advice that she had given them.

"Sharing a bathroom always leads to trouble," had been her first words of wisdom. "You must have a bathroom each. And Elena must have a kitchen that works. No cupboards, just big drawers, so you can find what you want without having to move anything. Two dishwashers; one just for glasses so they don't smear, and both of them built in at chest height so you don't have to bend over to load and unload. These may seem like little details, but they're important."

Elena seemed to be ready to go through Coco's ideas and suggestions for the rest of the house, but Reboul held up his hand to stop her somewhere between the bedroom and the living room. "I can see she hasn't changed," he said with a smile. "She always did like telling people what to do."

"But she knows what she's talking about," said Elena. "What can I say? It's so far so good."

Long may that last, thought Reboul, as he recalled the interminable and often frustrating meetings with his architect when renovating Le Pharo.

CHAPTER 10

The Fitzgeralds were now comfortably installed in their suite at the Plaza Athénée. This was Kathy's favorite hotel in Paris, not only for its elegance and excellent service, but also because of its convenient proximity to the temptations of the Avenue Montaigne. Each morning, after a light breakfast and a brisk session with Roberta ("Call me Bobbie"), her personal trainer, she would head out to the boutiques, her American Express card poised in expectation, and spend the hours until lunchtime choosing, trying on, and buying what she liked to think of as essential equipment for her casual French summer: dresses, caftans, Panama hats, swimsuits, the occasional handbag, and a selection of the latest beach jewelry. This had been her habit for the past two or three years, and she was now known to many of the sales assistants along the avenue; not just known, but deeply loved, as her budget was apparently limitless.

It hadn't taken her husband, Fitz, very long to discover that he had neither the stamina nor the interest for high-intensity shopping, and his mornings were spent in their suite with a cigar and his iPad, nursing his business interests around the world. At the end of the morning he and Kathy would meet for lunch. And today they had a lunch invitation. It had come from Coco's father, Alex, who would be arriving on the Riviera in a few days. Coco had suggested that the Fitzgeralds might enjoy getting to know him quietly before they all got caught up in the social whirl.

When they arrived at the Bistrot de Paris, they were taken to a table in the corner where their host was waiting. A stocky, well-tailored man in his late sixties, Alex had his daughter's dark coloring and, it quickly became obvious, his daughter's charm. He fussed over the Fitzgeralds and made sure they were comfortable. Champagne appeared, and Alex offered a toast.

"To Coco's favorite clients, the Fitzgeralds. If only they were all like you."

After that, conversation flowed easily. The two men started by exchanging a few credentials. Fitz mentioned his racehorses and his apartment on Central Park South; Alex countered with his collection of Impressionist paintings and his villa in Thailand. In this way, it was established that this was a meeting of equals, and that each was a man of taste and substance. Kathy told Coco later that it was like watching two tennis pros warming up.

By the time coffee arrived, an observer might have thought that the three of them were old friends. Arrangements were made to meet again on the Riviera. Alex just *had* to see the house on Cap Ferrat, so he and Coco *must* come over for dinner. As they parted company outside the restaurant, all of them felt that it had been a most pleasant and worthwhile meeting.

Kathy reported back to Coco on the phone that afternoon. "He's so charming, your dad. And Fitz really liked him — isn't that great? So we're all going to get together when we come down."

After Coco had made the appropriate noises, the conversation turned to the Fitzgeralds' party, and the all-important guest list. Coco had put together the names and brief descriptions of a dozen couples to add to the group of old American faithfuls on the existing list, and not surprisingly, several of these suggestions were Coco's clients. She had decided to include Elena and Sam, whose qualifications — the right age, amusing, and fluent in English — were impeccable. Kathy was delighted, and it was agreed that she and Coco would have what she called a working lunch as soon as she and Fitz had arrived on Cap Ferrat.

Elena and Sam had fallen into an instructive and enjoyable routine. Two or three mornings a week they would walk over to their house to check on its progress and to admire whatever had been done since their previous visit. They had quickly come to like and rely on Claude, the *chef de chantier,* who had worked with Coco for many years. He was a wiry, sun-wrinkled little man who had come up through the ranks of artisans, learning at every stage; masonry, plumbing, electricity — he had mastered them all, and more. If you weren't in a hurry, Coco had said, he could build you a house single-handed.

It was Claude who had initiated them into the pros and cons of polished concrete for the floors and the virtues of *tadelakt,* a waterproof, lime-based plaster, for the showers. He was an authority on everything from carpentry to ironwork; he revealed the secrets of aging new stonework until it achieved an eighteenth-century complexion;

he advised on the most effective protection of roof tiles from the brutal force of the Mistral. All this he passed on to Elena and Sam through a pungent haze of the cigarette smoke that came from his ever-present Gauloise while they pored, for the hundredth time, over the house plans that Coco had drawn up.

Having had their architectural fix, Elena and Sam would have lunch at Chez Marcel, on the Vieux Port, and then go back to Le Pharo for a swim and a siesta before bringing Reboul up to date. In this way the days passed very pleasantly. Elena had almost forgotten what an insurance office looked like, Sam was working on his French, and they were both enjoying exploring the towns and villages along the coast.

Having no pressing business to attend to — apart, of course, from the house — Sam found himself becoming more and more intrigued by what he had come to think of as a series of perfect crimes. These were the unsolved jewel robberies, such as the Castellaci heist that had cost Knox Insurance so dear. The work of professionals, Sam had no doubt, but how had they done it without leaving any clues? He wanted to find out more, and to do that he needed help: to start with, it would be useful to see and compare the police reports that had been filed after each of the unsolved robberies. Perhaps he could ask Reboul to persuade his friend Hervé to get hold of them.

But idle curiosity wasn't going to be enough to gain access to official police files. There would have to be another, more serious reason, and it came to him one afternoon while he and Elena were lying by the pool. It was time, he thought, for him to get himself a job, and he knew exactly where to get it. He leaned over and planted a kiss on Elena's bare stomach to distract her from the copy of *Salut!* magazine that Philippe had given her.

She looked at him over the top of her sunglasses, and smiled. "Is that a hint?"

"Not exactly," said Sam. "It's a business idea." And he took her through what he had in mind.

At first, Elena was skeptical. "Let me get this straight," she said. "You want me to get Frank Knox to hire you as his chief claims inspector in Europe?"

"Temporary, and unpaid. All I want is a letter from him, on Knox stationery, instructing me to pursue all lines of investigation relating to the Castellaci robbery. He needn't worry about the business cards; I'll get those done over here. With them and the letter, I'll have something official to show Hervé and his police buddies."

Elena shrugged. "Well, I guess it might work, and it won't do any harm."

She dropped her magazine, put her hand on the back of Sam's neck, and began to guide his head back down to her stomach. "Now, where were we?"

When Sam explained his idea that evening, Reboul was amused, and less skeptical than Elena had been. "It's true, of course, that we French love official-looking pieces of paper. But, my dear Sam, what do you expect to achieve with all this?"

"I'm not sure exactly. But as you know, professional crime has been a hobby of mine for years, and I find those robberies fascinating. Three of them, all perfect. Were they all done by the same guy? How did he do it? What did he do with the jewels?"

"And you don't think the police have asked themselves the same questions?"

"I'm sure they have. But they don't seem to have come up with any answers. Of course, it may be that these robberies weren't big enough to be interesting."

"What do you mean?"

"Well, don't forget what else has been going on. In 2009 — twenty million dollars' worth of jewels stolen from Cartier in Cannes. In 2010 — seven million stolen from a jewelry dealer near Marseille. In 2013 — one hundred and thirty-six million stolen from a diamond exhibition in Cannes. I guess the police have been concentrating on the big numbers, and not those little jobs that were done for a measly two or three million."

Reboul shrugged. "Who knows? Anyway, once you have the letter from Knox, I'll ask Hervé to see what he can do. Tell me again, where did your measly little robberies take place?"

"According to what Hervé told us when he was here the other night, there was one in Monaco, two or three years ago; another one, eighteen months later, in Antibes; and now this one in Nice. So I'd imagine that they wouldn't all come under the same police jurisdiction."

"That would be too easy." Reboul smiled. "I can see this might get complicated. Are you sure you wouldn't like to spend your time on something simple instead? *Boules?* Fishing? Deep-sea diving?"

CHAPTER 11

Fitzgerald was, as billionaires go, a simple and unpretentious man. But he had to admit that he relished the little ceremony of welcome performed on his arrival each summer by the staff of his house on Cap Ferrat. There were five of them: Monique, the cook; Odette, the housemaid; Jean-Pierre, the chauffeur; Émile, the head gardener; and Guillaume, his young assistant. Having been warned well in advance of the precise time of the Fitzgeralds' arrival, these five would be waiting in line outside the house to duck their heads in greeting, wish monsieur and madame *bonnes vacances,* and deal with the small mountain of luggage that had accompanied them.

A little later, Émile would escort Fitz and Kathy around the garden and point out the freshly shaved lawns, the freshly barbered palm trees, the year's new plantings, and the spectacular flower beds scattered throughout the grounds. Roberta would be busy in the pool house checking the exercise equipment, Monique would be hard at work in the kitchen stuffing *courgette* flowers for dinner that evening, and Odette would be unpacking the Fitzgeralds' clothes and hanging them in lavender-scented closets. This perfectly organized activity was a source of great pleasure to both Kathy and Fitz. It made them feel at home.

The garden tour over, they were sitting on the main terrace, going over their plans for the next few days.

"When are they all arriving?" asked Fitz. This year, there were three couples — their oldest and best friends from New York — who would be their houseguests for the summer.

Kathy consulted her iPad. "The Hoffmans and the Dillons are traveling together, and they'll be here next week; the Greenbergs are stopping off in London on the way, and they won't be arriving until that weekend. So we have a few days to ourselves."

"Great. I can do that meeting in Monaco before the fun starts." He saw that Kathy looked puzzled. "The guys from the bank need to go over some stuff that they didn't want to put in an e-mail. I guess I forgot to tell you because I know it's not your kind of thing; a few hours of numbers and not many jokes."

Kathy tried not to shudder at the thought. While she approved wholeheartedly of Fitz being rich, it was the end result she liked. The process of getting there, with its endless meetings and orgies of calculation, she found extremely boring. She leaned over and patted his cheek. "You're a sweetheart. Tell me when you're going, and I'll do my lunch with Coco."

The cards were printed on thick, buff-colored stock:

KNOX INSURANCE
Sam Levitt
European Claims Inspector

Sam ran his thumb over one of them, feeling the subtle engraving. The printer in Marseille that Reboul had recommended had done a first-class job, luxurious but tasteful, and perfect for a senior insurance executive. Once the letter from Frank Knox arrived, Sam could start work.

He knew that his main problem was going to be language. Although his French was improving daily, it wasn't good enough to deal with the various police officers whom he hoped to talk to, or to fully understand crime scene reports. These, as he knew from past experience in Los Angeles, were likely to be filled with official phraseology that was often difficult to understand even in English. It wasn't long before he realized that what he needed was an interpreter. Someone bilingual, obviously, and also smart, and preferably sympathetic to the investigation.

It had to be Philippe.

He picked up on the first ring. "Philippe, it's me. Sam."

"My friend, you don't have to tell me. We're living in the twenty-first century. Your name's on the screen. What can I do for you?"

"You can let me buy you lunch. I have an idea."

They agreed to meet at Chez Marcel the next day, which gave Sam a little time to work on his sales pitch. Philippe was a busy man, cruising up and down the coast to cover the doings of the beautiful people, and it would take something special to distract him.

Sam had asked Elena if she wanted to join them for lunch, but she told him she was far too busy. She was meeting Coco at the house to go over the choice of colors for

111

floors, walls, and shutters. In any case, she said, it would do Sam and Philippe good to have a boys' lunch. They could leer at the girls and swap risqué jokes.

Sam had by now become a regular at Chez Marcel, and he was treated to a regular's welcome. There was a double kiss from Julie, the chef's wife, and personal greetings from Serge, the chef himself, who had emerged from the kitchen, wiping his hands on his apron and full of enthusiasm for the dish of the day. Julie's Italian cousin from the Piedmont was visiting, and in his honor Serge had prepared *vitello tonnato,* which, he said, was so good it could make a grown man weep with pleasure.

Sam still had his nose in the wine list when Philippe appeared, cell phone planted in his ear and sunglasses perched on top of his head. Today he had abandoned his jeans and white jacket in favor of black silk sweatpants and a *Salut!* T-shirt.

"What do you think?" he asked Sam as he finished his call and pointed to the scarlet logo on his chest. "We're going to give sets of these T-shirts to the club bartenders along the coast, one white, one black, one blue. Pretty cool, eh?"

Julie came over to their table with menus, but Sam had already decided for both of them. "How could we resist? We'll have the *plat du jour,* and maybe something to drink. What would you suggest for the wine?"

"Arneis, if you want to drink Italian. It's perfect with the *vitello.*"

"Arneis it is."

Philippe looked up from his cell phone, eyebrows raised. "OK, my friend. What's this idea?"

"I'm hoping I've got an exclusive story for you, but you're going to have to work for it. First, let me give you a little background. I guess you've read about all these jewel robberies along the coast? And I imagine that jewelry is something that interests your readers?"

"Of course. The bigger the better."

"Well, there are three robberies that you won't have read about. Three perfect crimes, all unsolved. One in Antibes, one in Monaco, one in Nice. In other words, all in your patch."

The wine came, and was duly tasted and admired.

Sam could tell that he now had the attention of his audience, because Philippe had finally put away his cell phone. "What I've decided to do is to take a close look at these robberies. They were obviously done by professionals; maybe the same professionals

113

did all three. Anyway, I'm intrigued. I'd like to talk to the police, check out their reports, and see if I can find anything."

Philippe was shaking his head. "What makes you think the police will talk to you?"

Sam took out one of his new business cards and slid it across the table. "I am the officially accredited representative of a major U.S. insurance company, with clients in France."

Philippe studied it and shrugged. "That's a start, I guess."

"But it's not enough. My French is still worse than shaky, and so I'll need an interpreter." He raised his glass to Philippe. "And who better than you?"

Philippe sat back, his head cocked to one side, his brow furrowed, hardly the picture of enthusiasm.

"Here's the interesting part," said Sam. "What's in it for you. For a start, you get to make friends with three sets of cops along the coast. I don't have to tell you how useful they could be as sources of inside information when your celebrities get caught doing something dumb — dope, booze, car crashes, fistfights in nightclubs, that kind of thing. The stuff your readers love."

Sam paused to let the thought sink in.

"Even if that's all you get, it would be worth your time. But let's say we get lucky, and we come up with something that helps to solve the robberies." He raised his glass again. "You will have the exclusive to a story that will make waves all the way from here to Monaco."

Over the *vitello tonnato,* which prompted Philippe to make a quick trip to the kitchen, where he kissed his fingers several times to the chef, Sam filled in more details. Over the *pain perdu,* with sliced strawberries and a healthy hint of Grand Marnier, he mentioned the possibility of help from Hervé. By the time they had finished coffee, Sam had a partner.

When he got back to Le Pharo, he found Elena and Reboul sitting on the terrace, a selection of color charts and fabric swatches on the table in front of them. Reboul had a slightly bemused expression, and was visibly relieved to be able to take a break from the subtleties of interior decoration.

"Ah, Sam. How was your lunch?"

"Very good. Philippe's agreed to work with me." He bent down to kiss the top of Elena's head. "Isn't that great?"

Elena looked up at him, her mind clearly elsewhere. "Don't you think a very pale beige would be just right for the bedroom?"

CHAPTER 12

After his lunch with Sam at Chez Marcel, Philippe found himself with conflicting thoughts. He felt that there was next to no chance of Sam succeeding where three police forces had failed. Yet over the years he had seen his friend plunge into several unpromising situations — a couple of times in Marseille, and once in Corsica. Each time, he had come out on top. Why not this time? And, Philippe had to admit, it would make a hell of a story. A *Salut!* exclusive, syndicated worldwide, wherever diamonds were worn and stolen. It certainly wouldn't hurt his career.

There was, of course, the problem of his regular job as chronicler of the fabulous activities of *les people.* The season had begun, and before long the usual mixture of wretched excess — drunkenness, cocaine overdoses, fornication in the men's room — would start to yield promising material. He couldn't afford to miss that, as he had pointed out at lunch. Sam had been most understanding, although a little flippant. Who am I, he had said, to interfere with the sacred bond between journalist and reader? So they had agreed that *Salut!* came first, and Philippe's duties as interpreter and collaborator would have to fit in.

As a first step Philippe decided to pick the brains of Louis, a trusted contact from his previous job as a newspaper reporter for *La Provence.* Louis was one of those old-fashioned policemen who believed in old-fashioned methods. He preferred face-to-face conversations to e-mails and phone calls, and claimed that there was nothing more effective, when gathering information, than pounding the streets, collecting gossip picked up from bartenders and ladies of the night, and generally, as he put it, "sniffing the air." It was a technique that had served him well during his twenty-seven years on the force.

He and Philippe had agreed to meet at the Bar Saint-Charles, near the train station. It was dark and discreet, and the bartender's generous hand when pouring *pastis* had made it a popular spot for Marseille's thirsty policemen. When Philippe arrived, Louis was already leaning against the bar, studying a copy of *L'Équipe* to see if the Tour de France was likely to be won, yet again, by an impertinent foreigner.

"Loulou! Sorry I'm late. How are things? *Ça va?*"

The big policeman straightened up, smiled and nodded. "*Oui, oui, ça va.* Good to see you. Now, is this business or pleasure?"

"Business," said Philippe. "So I'm buying. What's it to be?"

Loulou allowed himself to be persuaded to have a *pastis,* and the two men settled at a table in the corner.

Philippe went through it all — the three perfect robberies, the lack of clues, the baffled policemen, and his friend Sam, the insurance executive from the States — while Loulou listened intently.

"So that's where we are at the moment," said Philippe. "We're going to get the crime scene reports, but I don't think they're going to tell us much. So I'm wondering if you know one of the guys in Antibes or Monaco or Nice who could help. We'd love to talk to someone involved with the investigations."

Loulou grunted. "That's like asking if I know any of the guys on Mars. We usually stick to our own turf. God knows there's enough trouble here without getting involved in other people's problems." He rubbed his chin, looked at his empty glass, and sighed. "Evaporation. The older I get, the more quickly it happens."

A second *pastis* was ordered, which seemed to stimulate Loulou's memory. "Come to think of it," he said, "I did have some dealings with some guys in Nice a couple of years ago. I'll make a few calls."

Sam reread the letter that had just arrived, written on official Knox Insurance paper and signed by Frank A. Knox, identified as the president. It was a small masterpiece of bureaucratic pomposity, instructing Sam to use his best efforts to establish the precise details of the robberies that were causing "such concern in American insurance circles." Perfect. He made a mental note to have a case of Champagne delivered to Knox. Now that he had his fake credentials, he could start work.

He showed the letter to Reboul, who shared Sam's fascination with the robberies. "This letter is fine," he said, "but it would help if we had something official from the French side. How would you like a letter from a senior officer of the Marseille police requesting that his colleagues provide you tance?"

"Hervé? Would he do that for me?"

Reboul grinned. "He'll do it for me. And you could show your gratitude in a way that he'd find most acceptable. Those cigars that you brought back from Jamaica and we put in the humidor in the wine cellar?"

"The Belicosos Finos?"

"Hervé loves a good cigar. A box would make him extremely happy. And co-operative." Reboul shrugged. "We all have our little *faiblesses.*"

As it happened, Hervé didn't need much persuasion when he came by that evening. He had already met Sam and liked him, and he found Sam's interest in the robberies amusing, even if his ambitions of solving them were wildly optimistic. But then, he was American, and it was well known — and perhaps envied by the pessimistic French — that all Americans were optimists.

The *rosé* was served. Sam produced and opened a box of cigars, and passed it to Hervé, who chose a cigar, inspected the band, squeezed the cigar gently, and sniffed it. Then he held it up against one ear and rolled it between his fingers. "Listening to the band," he said. "One can always hear if a cigar is too dry. This is excellent." He trimmed off the end and lit the cigar, inspecting the tip to make sure that it was an even, glowing red. The ritual concluded to his satisfaction, he leaned back, wreathed in smiles and fragrant smoke.

Sam went through his story, with Hervé nodding but saying nothing, which gave Sam the feeling that he was somehow being interrogated. He finished by showing Hervé the letter from Knox. "Francis suggested that I could use another letter, perhaps from an eminent senior member of the Marseille police, requesting cooperation."

Hervé nodded again. "I see. And you feel that would make a difference?"

"Absolutely. It would establish me as someone to be taken seriously here in France."

Hervé took a long, thoughtful pull of his cigar. "Well, I'd be happy to do that, as long as you keep me informed of any progress that you make. To be frank, I don't think you'll get anywhere." He shrugged. "But if you should turn up anything, I want to be the first to know, *d'accord?*"

"I promise," said Sam. "And I hope you will accept these cigars as a mark of my gratitude for your help."

The beam on Hervé's face was answer enough.

■ ■ ■ ■

It was lunchtime on Cap Ferrat, once the domain of King Leopold of the Belgians, and now, after Monaco, the most expensive real estate on the coast. Kathy Fitzgerald had invited Coco to come over, and there were many important subjects to discuss. First, the houseguests would need to know the names of the support group that was so essential whenever and wherever the rich go on vacation: hairdressers and manicurists, the latest fashionable chef, tai chi instructors, masseuses, and, most crucial of all, a doctor who spoke English. There was also an obligatory update on the Riviera gossip, and finally, the guest list for the upcoming party.

Monique, the Fitzgeralds' cook, had prepared what Kathy called a *snack de luxe* lunch: roasted mixed vegetables with rosemary and thyme, and a mousse of goat cheese with balsamic vinegar. Thus fortified, the ladies turned their attention to the main business of the day, the party. Coco went through the list she had prepared of possible guests: Armand and Edouard, a charming gay couple who worked in the world of fashion in Paris; Nina de Montfort, a serial heiress, and her latest youthful admirer; the Osbornes, Coco's young English clients; Alain Laffont, who played eight-goal handicap polo when he wasn't busy selling high-end real estate, and his girlfriend Stanislavska, the Czech model; Hubert, a cosmetic surgeon, and his wife Éloise (known rather unkindly to some as Madame Botox); Coco's father, Alex, of course; and Elena and Sam. "Sounds like a fun group," said Kathy. "And they all speak English? I don't want any French wallflowers."

Coco laughed. "Don't worry. They all speak English, and none of them except my father is over forty. Oh, and Nina — her real age is a state secret; she's been thirty-nine for years. I think you'll really get on with Elena and Sam — they're American, and I'm fixing up a little house they've bought near Marseille. So they're almost neighbors."

"That's great. Could I ask you to take care of the invitations? For the twenty-third?"

"Of course."

Later that afternoon, Coco started making her calls. The combination of Cap Ferrat and wealthy Americans appealed, for different reasons, to all the names on her list, and by the time she called Elena she hadn't had a single refusal.

"I'm sure you'll have a good time," she said to Elena. "Kathy and Fitz are nice people, and the other guests are — well, they're interesting. I know all of them, and it should be an amusing evening."

When Elena passed on the news to Sam, he immediately thought of Philippe. "High society on the Riviera," he said. "They might like to see themselves in *Salut!* What do you think?"

CHAPTER 13

Sam's nostrils twitched, and he opened one bleary eye to see, on the bedside table, a tray with a large cup of *café crème* and a plump croissant.

Elena emerged from the bathroom, dressed and brisk and clearly impatient for the day to begin. "In case you were wondering," she said, "I was the breakfast fairy. I went down to the kitchen when I woke up."

Sam sat up, took a bite of his croissant, and reached for the coffee. "You're a princess. Tell me, are we in a hurry, or is it just that you couldn't sleep?"

"We have an early meeting with Coco, remember?"

He saw that Elena was tapping her watch. "OK, OK, I'm coming."

They had fallen into the habit of walking from Le Pharo to their house, a twenty-five-minute stroll, mostly along a narrow, rocky path. It was still too early for the sun to be any more than pleasantly warm. The sea was without a wrinkle, and the Marseille seagulls — as big as geese, the locals would tell you — were wheeling and floating in the deep blue sky.

"This beats commuting," said Sam. "What's on the menu this morning?"

"Coco wants to show us an antique front door she's found, and she'd like you to see the finish she's suggesting for your shower. Then there's the usual stack of details to go over for the kitchen. And I have to decide where I want the bidet in my bathroom."

As they got closer, they could hear their house being worked on before they could see it — the rasp of a stonecutter trimming a flagstone, the grumbling monotone of the cement mixer, the occasional shout from the workmen, snatches of music coming from a radio.

"You're enjoying all this," said Sam. "I'm glad you and Coco are getting along."

"She's terrific. She explains everything, and she's great on all the details. I think we got lucky."

They arrived at the house to find Coco, dressed for work as usual in white dungarees, supervising two workmen who had unloaded the antique door from their truck and were now leaning it up against the wall

126

next to the empty doorway. Coco was considering it, head cocked to one side, when she realized that her clients had arrived.

"I think that works," she said, coming over for the exchange of good-morning kisses. "Do you like it? My father found it in Paris. He's taking quite an interest in my work recently."

It was a simple, substantial door that dated, so Coco thought, from the late eighteenth century. The years had been kind to the wood, a rich, dark blond oak, and it might have been made to complement the sun-bleached walls of the house. Elena and Sam both loved it.

"By the time you come again we'll have put it up. But it was missing one thing," said Coco. She went over and picked up an object that was propped against the door. "Here — a little housewarming gift." It was a bronze door-knocker in the form of a slender female hand, hinged at the wrist, holding a bronze ball. "It's a bit later than the door — I guess nineteenth century — but I think they go well together."

The rest of the morning passed in a pleasant blur of details and suggestions, all of which were covered in a list that Coco had prepared for them, and by the time they were getting ready to go and find some lunch they had, once again, mentally moved in.

Elena took a photograph of Sam holding up the door-knocker to see how it looked against the door. "I can't believe how fast the work is going," she said. "Are you happy with everything?"

Sam nodded and grinned. "Especially your bidet. I'm thrilled with your bidet."

Philippe's call came as they were finishing a café lunch down by the Vieux Port. "Here's a bit of luck," he said. "My friend Loulou knows one of the guys in Nice who worked on the Castellaci case, so I'm hoping we can make a start there. He's going to get us all the paperwork."

"Very good," said Sam. "How are you fixed for time?"

"This week's shot. There's a new nightclub opening in Cannes, a charity ball in Monte Carlo, and then down to Saint-Tropez for a swimsuit-and-Champagne fashion show on the beach, where there's always a good chance of accidental nudity."

"Accidental?"

"You'd be amazed how often accidents happen when there's a camera around. Anyway, the week after that should be less busy. I'll call Loulou's guy and see if I can make an appointment for us."

Sam was shaking his head as he finished the call. "I think Philippe's found his vocation. He's now a student of accidental nudity."

Alex Dumas picked up a cab at Nice Airport for the short trip to Le Negresco. Thanks to Coco's influence, a suite had been made available to him for the price of a single room, and despite the fact that he was an extremely wealthy man, modest savings like this were important to him. He had never forgotten those early poverty-stricken days when he had struggled for every cent. His father, a minor civil servant, had died young, leaving Alex to supplement the small family income. He'd worked as a waiter and a bartender before striking up an instant rapport with one of his customers, an elderly antique dealer who promptly hired him as an assistant. The dealer felt he'd found a son. Alex felt he'd found a father. He subsequently inherited the business, and never looked back.

Coco had prepared the hotel staff for her father's visit, and he was treated like an old and valued client. The doorman, in his Negresco uniform of top hat and scarlet and blue frock coat, took Dumas's suitcase from the taxi and was evidently delighted to see him. So was the welcoming committee at the front desk. Even the bellboy who took the suitcase up to his suite seemed to have been counting the moments until his arrival.

As for his accommodation, he could hardly have hoped for anything better. The view alone — of the Promenade des Anglais and the endless blue of the Mediterranean — was, he thought, worth the cost of the suite. And someone had left an ice bucket and a bottle of Dom Perignon on the coffee table. How kind and thoughtful. Dumas opened the envelope that had been delivered with the Champagne. The note inside was from Coco: *Papa — Save some of this for me. I'll be with you about six-thirty. C xx.*

In her office in another part of the hotel, Coco was on the phone to Kathy Fitzgerald. Their calls had become more and more frequent — they spoke at least once a day — as Coco did what she could to help Kathy with the preparations for the party.

"Something's come up," said Coco, "which might be fun. I was talking to Elena and Sam, those nice Americans. They have a friend, Philippe, who is the Riviera correspondent for *Salut!* — you know, that glossy social magazine. Sam said he thought that Philippe would love to come with his photographer and do a piece on your party. How do you feel about that?"

Kathy hesitated for at least two seconds. "Wow! What a great souvenir of the evening. Could you fix that up?"

"Of course. I think Philippe would want to meet you before the party. Would that be OK?"

"Sure — and Coco, thanks so much for all your help. I really appreciate it."

Sam's early-evening call found Philippe and Mimi in the empty gloom of Le Club Croisette, the most recent addition to the nightlife of Cannes. As Philippe had explained to the club's owner, Mimi always liked to take a quick look at the space before she came in to do the shoot. The owner was delivering a breathless, and seemingly endless, recital of all the celebrities who had been invited to the club's opening later that night. The call, brief as it was, came as a welcome interruption.

"Practicing your pole dancing for tonight? How's the club?"

"It's fine. But Sam, I'm a little busy right now."

"I'll make it quick. Keep the evening of the twenty-third free. We've got a nice little gig for you. I'll call you later."

Philippe turned back to the club's owner. "Do you think she's really going to come, Carla Bruni?"

When their reconnaissance ended, Mimi and Philippe were having an early dinner at Miramar Plage, a beach restaurant on the Croisette.

"Well," said Philippe, "what did you think of it?"

Mimi took a sip of wine and looked out at the sun slipping down toward the horizon. "I don't know. Compared to this . . ." — she waved an arm at the view — "it's difficult to get excited about a dark hole in the ground, no matter how much they've spent tarting it up to make it look glamorous. These places are always depressing when they're empty; they look better when they're jammed with people. But don't worry — I'm sure I'll get some good shots."

Philippe's phone rang. It was Sam calling back with a few details of the Fitzgerald party, and the guests whom Coco had invited. "Sounds like an interesting bunch of people," he said, "and I know that Elena would love to see Mimi again, but you've been keeping her so busy lately. How about it?"

Philippe thought for a moment. The party

sounded a little thin on major celebrities, but the glamour of Cap Ferrat was always a plus, and rich Americans having a good time would be a change from Europeans and Russians misbehaving. "OK," he said. "Why not?"

CHAPTER 14

Despite the demands placed on him as the chronicler of *les people,* Philippe found that he still had time to think about his scoop — the exclusive revelation of the true story behind the unsolved robberies. This in turn led him to refine an idea that had been in the back of his mind for some time: a series that featured the homes of the rich and famous. Now, he thought, the robberies could add another dimension to that idea. It was obvious that the victims of those robberies were, if not famous, certainly rich. And the mysterious circumstances surrounding the robberies had the makings of the kind of story that the readers of *Salut!* would find irresistible.

The problem, of course, would be persuading the owners to give him access to their homes. His old ally, human nature, would help; he was still astonished that the lure of celebrity was potent enough to make people agree to all kinds of invasions of their privacy. But this time, he would probably need something more, a rational excuse for them to throw open their front doors. It was time, he decided, to share his thoughts with Sam.

It was the morning after the swimsuit fashion show at Saint-Tropez when they met for coffee at Le Pharo.

"How was it?" said Sam.

Philippe shook his head. "Amazing. After the first half-hour the bikini tops started dropping like leaves in autumn. Perfectly tanned bosoms everywhere — you'd have loved it."

Sam grinned. "Sounds like a tough job, but I guess somebody had to do it. Now, what's this idea you want to talk about?"

After Philippe had finished, Sam was silent and thoughtful for a few moments. "Well," he said finally, "it's not a bad idea, but I don't know if the owners would want to be reminded of a lousy experience. You're right — we need to find a serious reason to get them to let you in."

"You two look like you're plotting. Can I join in?" It was Elena, back from a morning swim and desperate for coffee. She filled a cup from the *cafetière* and looked at them expectantly. Sam took her through Phi-

135

lippe's idea, and repeated his own reaction.

Elena nodded. "I can see the problem. I suppose the obvious thing to do would be to give it a try — you know, ask them how they feel about having their homes photographed."

Sam nodded slowly and turned to Philippe. "Are you thinking what I'm thinking?" Philippe looked blank. "Our favorite insurance executive, Ms. Morales, already knows two of the victims — that couple in Nice, the Castellacis. How about asking them?" They both looked at Elena.

She shook her head. "We could try. But why would they want to say yes? What's in it for them?"

Sam sighed. "That's the big question. The last thing they would want, I guess, is to become celebrities for being robbed. And let's not forget the main reason for wanting to get into these places is not — forgive me, Philippe — to do an article for *Salut!* It's to see if we can pick up anything that would help us get somewhere with these robberies."

Elena was frowning as she removed her sunglasses and, in a somewhat absentminded way, started to polish them on the corner of her towel. "I'm beginning to get an idea," she said. "Supposing I asked the

Castellacis if I could introduce them to Knox Insurance's top investigator, the European claims inspector, Mr. Sam Levitt? And supposing Mr. Levitt was working on a new security project that would make homes more burglar-proof than they had ever been before?"

"Isn't it a little late for that?" said Sam. "I mean, the thief has already paid them a visit. The diamonds are gone. The damage has already been done."

"Of course. But the diamonds will probably be replaced. And besides, they have other stuff that has to be insured. We could tell the Castellacis that if they agree to help us, we would install the new system for free once it's been perfected. We might also say there's a chance that their premium would be reduced, which would appeal to that miserable little bastard of a husband."

Sam leaned over and kissed her. "There's nothing I love more than an intelligent woman with great legs and criminal tendencies."

The rest of the morning was spent discussing and elaborating Elena's idea, and by the time Reboul's chef came out shortly after noon to count the heads for lunch, they all felt that they had something to work with. As long as the Castellacis could be persuaded to agree.

Reboul himself had come back after a hard morning of banging heads in the office, and was delighted to find that he had three companions who could join him for lunch. He was in better spirits than they had seen him in for a long time, and the reason for this was revealed when the first glasses of *rosé* had made their appearance. His long-distance lady friend, Monica Chung, had agreed to take a break from her business in Hong Kong and spend the summer with him in Provence.

"I'm so happy for you," said Elena to Reboul as they made their way to the table. "I remember Monica. She's lovely."

"Not only that," said Reboul, "but she's a wonderful cook, so I'm hoping that Alphonse will let her into his kitchen from time to time."

And there was Alphonse, waiting for them at the head of the table. In addition to his duties as chef, he took great pleasure in announcing, often in great detail, what his guests were about to eat. This had led Sam to call him the Living Menu.

Alphonse tapped the rim of a wineglass with a knife. "Today, we start with a seasonal encouragement for the taste buds, a summer soup of chilled melon. The melons, to be sure, come from Cavaillon, melon capital of the world. And then to follow, a dish very popular with our friends in Corsica: *bresaola* — very fine slices of air-cured beef, served with olive oil, a sauce of melted Gorgonzola cheese, and baby roasted potatoes. And to finish, a two-tone chocolate mousse with a tiny whirl of vanilla on top. *Et voilà!*" After a short pause for applause, he returned to the kitchen.

Sam and Philippe brought Reboul up to date with their progress on the robberies; Elena brought him up to date with the progress on the house. By the time he left them having coffee on the terrace, he was almost giddy with information, and was looking forward to a peaceful afternoon in the office.

Philippe stretched, and looked at his watch. "I'm free for the rest of the day. Do you feel like showing me your new house?"

The antique door had been hung, the knocker attached, the windows fitted, and the exterior flagstones laid. Suddenly, the house had begun to look less like a bomb site and more like what a pompous real estate agent might describe as a desirable residence. Philippe couldn't get over the view, and became more and more thoughtful as he was shown around the inside of the house.

"What a wonderful spot," he said. "Are you going to have a housewarming party?"

"Certainly," said Sam. "The two of us, Mimi and you, and Francis. And maybe Alphonse in the kitchen. That's it."

"Of course," said Philippe. "I can understand that, even if I don't see much of it."

"What's that?"

"Low-profile behavior." There was a moment of hesitation before Philippe spoke again. "Would you think of making an exception? Mimi and I are going to get married in September, and this would be a sensational place for an after-wedding party."

Elena and Sam looked at each other, and they both smiled. "On one condition," said Elena. "We get invited."

It had been a more than usually tiring day for Coco — starting in Nice, with side trips to Marseille and Cassis — and she was suffering from an overdose of impatient clients and whining workmen. By the time she got back to her office that evening, all she wanted was complete silence and a glass of good red wine.

She slipped off her shoes, went out to the terrace, and sat down with a sigh of relief. As if on cue, her cell phone rang.

It was Kathy Fitzgerald, bubbling with gratitude. "It was *so* sweet of you to have that cute Monsieur Gregoire come around. He went through the whole house, just making sure that everything was OK. What a great guy."

Coco took a sip of wine to help her recover from her surprise. "I hope he wasn't a nuisance?"

"Not at all. He said that things could go wrong even when we weren't living in the house, and he wanted to make sure we hadn't moved back in and found problems." Kathy continued in this way for several minutes, praising Gregoire's conscientious attention to detail, his efficiency, and, of course, his cuteness.

Coco was shaking her head as she put down the phone. What the hell did he think he was doing? She thought of calling him, but abandoned the idea in favor of another glass of wine. Gregoire could wait until tomorrow.

CHAPTER 15

The three of them had gathered in Philippe's apartment, a block away from the Corniche, for a meeting of what Sam called the Marseille Sports and Social Club. At the top of the list of subjects to be discussed was the police report that Madame Castellaci had passed on to Elena after the robbery.

It made unexciting reading. The first page set the scene: address, owners' names, detailed description of the premises, date and approximate time of the robbery, estimated value of the stolen diamonds. With these formalities out of the way, it was time for page two, where the optimistic reader might have hoped to find some imaginative theories about how the thief had managed to enter the building, ransack the wall safe, and escape without leaving anything that resembled a clue. But imagination was in short supply, and this page merely catalogued the details of the security equipment, from the number and positioning of the electronic alarms to the impenetrable thickness of the door of the waterproof, fireproof wall safe. And then to the third and final page, rather grandly headed "Methodology and Conclusions."

This was a litany of officialese, describing what had been done in the course of the investigation. The members of the Castellaci domestic staff had been "extensively questioned," and their alibis had been "thoroughly verified." The premises had been "rigorously searched," unfortunately without finding anything except an empty safe; and so it went on, with one dead end followed by another. The conclusion, such as it was, stated that "further investigations will be conducted as and when appropriate."

"Well," said Sam, "that's about what we expected. And it doesn't get us anywhere. We'll see when we get the other two reports, but I guess they'll be pretty much the same." He turned to Elena. "Over to you, Madame Sherlock. It's time we tried your idea."

Elena nodded. "OK, but I'm not going to make the call with you two hanging over me. I need a little space. Philippe, where's your bathroom?"

Philippe showed her into the bathroom, apologizing for the lack of a comfortable chair.

Elena perched on the toilet seat. "This'll do fine — I'm not planning on a long stay. Could you close the door on your way out?"

Five minutes passed. Sam and Philippe, pacing up and down the living room, agreed that this was a hopeful sign. At least the Castellacis hadn't told Elena to get lost. And when, a few minutes later, she emerged from the bathroom, it was with a broad smile on her face.

"There you are, boys. If you need something done, ask a woman to do it. By the way, Philippe, it's time you changed those towels."

Philippe winced, then waved a hand at her, as if to say that he was far too busy to attend to minor domestic details.

"That's terrific. I want to hear all about it," said Sam, giving Elena a hug. "But not on an empty stomach. How about lunch?"

"How about Chez Marcel?"

Settled around a table on the restaurant terrace, the menus considered and dealt with, a bottle of Corsican *rosé* in the ice bucket, the postmortem on Elena's phone call could begin.

"Luckily," she said, "the housekeeper picked up the phone. If it had been the husband, I think he'd have told me to get lost. So now it's me and Madame Castellaci, and she's altogether more reasonable. We chatted for a couple of minutes, and she told me her husband's in New York this week for a linguine festival organized by the Italian tourist board. Bet you're both sorry you missed that." Elena paused for a sip of wine. "Then she asked me why I'd called, and I got going on the story. Sam, you'd have been embarrassed — although, knowing you, maybe not. I told her that one of the keenest brains in the insurance business had been sent over from L.A. with a brief to upgrade the security arrangements for all Knox clients in Europe. This is a man revered by other insurance executives who know him — and there are very few of those, because he prides himself on his personal discretion — for his ability to outthink the criminal mind. It is this exceptional talent that helps him provide such effective security solutions for his clients."

"Don't tell me," said Sam. "Then she asked where was he when we needed him."

"I didn't give her a chance. I went on to

say that this genius had just arrived in Nice, and would very much appreciate the opportunity to come with me and our CSP to see her." She looked at Sam and Philippe, clearly pleased to see their puzzled faces. "You boys wouldn't know what a CSP is, because I just made it up; it stands for 'crime scene photographer,' and it's our excuse for having Philippe with us. Anyway, she was all for it, and she suggested Thursday morning."

"What about the husband?"

"I asked. She said this would be a nice surprise for him."

Sam and Philippe raised their glasses to Elena just as Julie, the chef's wife, appeared with their first course. Guided by Philippe, they were having one of the Chez Marcel specialties, fried aubergines with a *coulis* of tomato and basil. And like all house specialties, this had to have a detailed presentation, delivered by Julie and translated by Philippe.

The aubergines are cut into thick slices, arranged in layers with salt from the Camargue between each layer, and left overnight to drain. In the morning, each slice of aubergine is dried, deep-fried in olive oil, and drained again on absorbent paper. Then, *la touche finale,* the slices are arranged in the shape of a daisy, with the *coulis* of tomato with fresh basil and olive oil poured into the middle. *Bon appétit!*

In unison, Philippe and Julie kissed their fingertips, glasses were refilled, and conversation was resumed.

Elena tasted her aubergine with a little sigh of satisfaction. "You'll have to dress for this visit, you know. Dark suit and a tie for you, Sam. And something a little more formal than a *Salut!* T-shirt for Philippe."

"What about you?" said Sam. "Shorts and high heels?"

"Of course. Isn't this delicious?"

And so were the courses that followed: simple but perfect lamb chops, with potatoes roasted, in the Provençal way, in olive oil; and to finish, homemade iced nougat with lavender honey from the local bees.

Over coffee, they were starting to go over the details of their meeting when Sam turned to Elena. "There's one thing that bothers me about all this," he said, "and that's how you feel about it. I mean, what we're doing may not qualify as a serious crime, but it's certainly misrepresentation, possibly fraud, and perhaps not what a well-brought-up young lady can feel comfortable with. Have you thought about that?"

Elena reached over to give Sam's hand a

squeeze. "Of course I have. But you have to remember all those years I've spent in the insurance business. I've found that clients lie all the time, and usually the richer they are the bigger the lies. That's not an excuse for doing what we're doing, but it's a reason. And here's another one: I'd be surprised if we didn't find that at least one of these three robberies was an inside job, a self-inflicted scam. Now, that's a crime, and I'd be happy to play a part in solving it. And besides — are we doing any real harm? I don't think so. In other words, to answer your question, I'm quite comfortable."

Madame Castellaci's housekeeper let them in and took them through to the living room, where madame was waiting to receive them. As instructed by Elena, Sam was in a dark-blue suit with a sober tie, and Philippe had forsaken his T-shirt for a respectable white linen jacket and freshly pressed jeans. Slung over his shoulder was Mimi's Nikon. Elena, in her business black, made the introductions.

"Very well," said Madame Castellaci. "Your colleague Ms. Morales has already explained the purpose of your visit. Where do you want to start?"

The tour of inspection began with the

safe. Sam, in his role of security expert, tested the combination lock and instructed Philippe to take photographs of the safe with its door open and closed. They then moved on to check the alarm devices and the wiring in each room and the level of protection provided by the windows and shutters, with Philippe taking photographs and Sam making copious notes as they moved through the house. An hour had gone by before they arrived back where they started, at the front door. Madame Castellaci had watched with interest but without comment until Sam put away his notebook.

"So," she said, "have you seen enough? Now what happens?"

Sam smiled. "A lot of thinking, and some research. You have a conventional alarm system. Unfortunately, a professional thief doesn't operate by conventional rules. Whoever robbed you will have studied all the existing systems, and worked out how to bypass them. You tell me that your system was installed four years ago; is that right?" Madame Castellaci nodded. "Well, I'm afraid that technology can change a lot in four years, and the fact is that the professional thief is usually one step ahead of the security industry. He also knows that very few people have their alarm systems checked and updated every year. How about you?"

"Well, we've been meaning to, but . . ."

"I know," said Sam. "As long as there aren't any obvious problems, people don't bother. But let me tell you about what I'm working on at the moment, with a company in California. It's a device no bigger than a pack of cigarettes that links you to your alarm system when you're away from your house. The slightest interference with the system will activate the device; a buzzer will sound, in your pocket or handbag, and you can immediately call the police. With luck, they'll get there while the thief is still busy."

"Won't he know that he's set something off?"

Sam shook his head. "The only person who will know is you. It may not be the ultimate solution, but it'll help, and the people in California are perfecting it right now. It should be available by Christmas."

"Sam, I'm impressed," said Elena. "Where did that idea come from?" They had stopped in at a café not far from the Castellaci house.

"Childhood research. I think it was in an old Dick Tracy comic book. Although, come to think of it, perhaps it was a techno bore I met last year in L.A. telling me how smart his new phone was. But I prefer to have Dick Tracy get the credit."

CHAPTER 16

Philippe and Mimi pulled up outside the Cap Ferrat house just before 10:00 a.m., the time that Sam had fixed for their visit. Kathy Fitzgerald, in a high state of excitement, was already waiting for them on the front terrace. She was waving as she came up to greet them.

"Hi! This is great!" A sudden horrifying thought made her pause and frown. "Do you *parler anglais*? Sam didn't say."

Philippe reassured her, perhaps exaggerating just a little his slight American accent, and introduced Mimi, who, he said "speaks better English than me."

"Than *I*," said Mimi, with a smile. Her English grammar was considerably more polished than Philippe's.

Kathy was visibly relieved. "That's great," she said again. "Now, I'm sure you guys would like a cup of coffee before we get started." She led the way to a table on the terrace where Odette, the Fitzgeralds' housemaid, was arranging cups, saucers, coffeepot, and croissants. The three of them settled down around the table for some discreet mutual inspection.

As Philippe said later, Kathy could have been nothing but a wealthy American: glossy blonde hair, immaculate complexion, wonderful teeth, the body of a twenty-year-old, and clothes that managed to look both casual and extremely expensive. Not to be outdone, Mimi was wearing what she called her society photographer's outfit — a black silk frock coat over a white T-shirt, white jeans, and white leather Tod's moccasins. Philippe had resisted the lure of his *Salut!* T-shirts in favor of a dark-blue cotton suit, blue-and-white striped shirt, and, that badge of urban cool, a three-day growth of stubble.

"OK," said Kathy. "Let's start outside. On the night, all the terraces around the house will be lit with those flaming torches you see in Robin Hood movies. There'll be a bar down there by that far wall, and a cute little band we found in Nice will be playing for anyone who wants to dance. We'll be serving dinner on the main terrace. God forbid it should rain, but if it does we'll have tables inside. There's plenty of space. Shall we take a look?"

She led them into the house and through double doors that opened onto the living room. Mimi and Philippe stopped at the threshold to take it in.

"Mon Dieu," said Mimi.

"Merde!" said Philippe, which prompted an elbow in the ribs from Mimi.

The reason for their surprise was the size of the room they were looking at. It was enormous, running the full length of the house, broken up into alcoves on each side. These areas were equipped for a variety of interests and diversions. There was a pool table, a king-sized flat-screen television, a backgammon table, a compact but well-stocked library, an equally well-stocked bar, and, in the center of the room, a quadrangle of huge sofas arranged around a pair of massive teak coffee tables. The room could have been a chaotic mess, but it had been so well thought out and arranged that you could almost forget how big it was.

"So you see," Kathy said, "even if it does rain, we have plenty of space for all the guests. This is our kind of everything room. Fitz and I each have our own little offices, of course, but we spend a lot of time in here when we're not outside."

"I can see why," said Philippe. "It's a great

room. Oh, you just mentioned your husband. I hope we're going to meet him before the party."

"Sure you will, but not this morning. He had to go to Monaco for a meeting. Now Mimi, what else would you like to see? The pool area, perhaps?"

"That would be good. And I'd like to take a look around all the terraces. In a setting like this, you never know where people might go. They drift, they have a drink here, they have a drink there — it's sometimes difficult to know where the action's going to be."

Kathy nodded, as if she knew only too well the trials of a society photographer's work. She turned to Philippe. "How about you, Philippe? Do you have any prepping to do?"

"I'd certainly like a guest list, so we don't spell any names wrong when the piece appears. And I'll need a few tips from you."

Kathy nodded again, thrilled to be part of the creative process. "Whatever you want."

"OK. Well, first, let me just say that *Salut!* isn't one of those magazines that specializes in hatchet jobs. You know the kind of thing: shots of some guy off in the bushes with another man's wife. Or anyone who is falling-down drunk. Or fistfights on the dance floor. We leave all that to what the

155

English call the gutter press. All we try to do is show attractive, interesting people in nice clothes having a good time."

"I am *so* pleased to hear that," said Kathy, who had experienced one or two misgivings about how the strangers she had invited would behave. Strangers or not, they were now promoted. "I mean, these people are *friends,* so I wouldn't want to upset them."

"Don't you worry. But here's where I'll need your help. You're going to have to warn us if any of your guests have — how can I put it — special requests."

Kathy's eyebrows went up at this; it sounded slightly suggestive. "Such as?"

Philippe grinned. "Nothing like that. But, for example, some ladies prefer to be photo-graphed from a certain angle; some men don't want to be photographed wearing their glasses, or holding a cigarette. These are details, but they're important. Mimi's very good at checking these things out, but she prefers unposed shots, which look more natural. So if you could whisper in her ear from time to time, it would be a great help."

"You got it," said Kathy.

The three of them then made a tour of the terraces surrounding the house and the pool area, with Mimi taking reference shots as they went. Kathy was almost skipping

156

with enthusiasm, convinced that this was going to be an evening to remember, and delighted to have found two such great people to work with. Definitely a darling couple.

During the drive back to Marseille, Mimi and Philippe were speculating, as they always did, about the evening's prospects. Would it be as bland as Philippe had suggested? What about the saucy goings-on that the readers of *Salut!* had come to expect?

"Let's not worry about that," said Philippe. "If we need to, we can always ask Elena and Sam to do something a little *risqué* to liven things up. Have you ever seen them do the tango?"

"That was before my time. When did you see that?"

"At a party when I was with them in L.A. Sensational."

Unaware that he was being considered for a star turn at the Fitzgeralds' party, Sam, with help from Reboul, was going through the other two police reports that Hervé had obtained. They were depressingly similar to the first report — the same meticulous formula, even the same vague, all-purpose conclusion.

Sam sat back, shaking his head. "Do you

think they all learn this at the police academy? Crime Scene Reporting 101?"

"My dear Sam," said Reboul, "remember that this is France. Anything and everything connected with the French bureaucracy has its official system with its official forms. These must be carefully completed, signed, countersigned, and stamped, before being filed and forgotten. This is a country where a relatively simple legal dispute can drag on for ten years. Don't count on learning much from official reports. I'm afraid you're going to have to look somewhere else for inspiration."

"Well, I know where I want to look. We've seen the Castellaci house, and I'd like to see the two other houses that were robbed. And, if possible, meet the owners. I guess what I'm looking for is a link. From what I know so far, there are basic similarities between all three robberies: no signs of breaking into the house, no signs of forcing the wall safes, nothing else stolen apart from the jewels, no clues. Now, if there had been just one robbery like that, I might suspect an inside job. But three? That, to me, suggests an organized, well-informed setup, perhaps a group, who have found a way through modern security systems. It happens."

Reboul was smiling as he leaned forward to pat Sam on the shoulder. "I'll see what I can do. But Sam, are you sure you want to spend your time on this? Wouldn't you rather be enjoying yourself with the lovely Elena?"

"The lovely Elena is having a great time with the house, and she's very happy that I've got something to keep me occupied. She knows that this business of the robberies fascinates me, and, as she's told me more than once, it means that I'm not always distracting her when she has vital plumbing decisions to make."

Reboul was still smiling as he looked at his watch. "It seems to me," he said, "that it's time for a glass of *rosé,* and I'll tell you something interesting and rather surprising. *Rosé* has become so popular in France that we're now drinking more than we produce, with the risk that we might have to import it to satisfy demand. Can you imagine that? How times have changed. I'm sure you've heard that old phrase that wine snobs love: '*Rosé* — no sooner made than drunk, no sooner drunk than pissed away.' You don't hear that so often nowadays. Anyway, dear Monica, over in Hong Kong, was so concerned about the thought of France running out of *rosé* that she rushed off to her local Chinese wine merchant and had him send me this."

Reaching into the refrigerator under the bar, Reboul produced a bottle of lurid pink liquid. Sharing the label with a drawing of China's famous wall were the words "GREAT WALL ROSE WINE, bottled by Huaxia Winery, Hebei, China."

"What do you think of that?" said Reboul, drawing the cork.

"I think Monica's having a little joke."

"Well, we won't know until we taste it."

"You first."

CHAPTER 17

Sam and Philippe had agreed to meet on the terrace of a café near the Vieux Port at 11:00 a.m., but it was close to 11:30 before Philippe showed up. He negotiated his way gingerly, like a blind man without his cane, through the small tables that were lined up on the terrace before settling, with a muffled moan, opposite Sam.

"Just been for your morning jog?"

Philippe winced. "Last night was this charity evening in aid of the distressed gentlewomen of Marseille. Some seriously rich people, an auction, a band, all the usual stuff. Anyway, they raised a lot of money and decided to turn it into a Champagne all-nighter, and Mimi and I didn't get home until five in the morning." Philippe signaled a waiter, and then, taking three aspirin out of his pocket, ordered a double espresso, a glass of water, and a shot of Calvados. "So that was my evening. How about you?"

"Chinese *rosé* and these police reports from the other two robberies." Sam tapped the reports on the table in front of him.

"How do they compare with the first one?"

"Almost identical. As Francis said to me, we're going to have to look somewhere else for inspiration."

There was a brief pause while Philippe administered the coffee, the aspirin, and, with a shudder, the Calvados. "*Ouf!* That's better. You know it's doing you good when it hurts." He reached over and took the reports. "Do we know where these other two places are?"

"Monaco and Antibes. The addresses and the owners' names are in the reports. So I guess we should try the routine that worked with the Castellacis. Now, judging by the names, the place in Monaco is owned by a French couple, the Rimbauds. And the owners of the place in Antibes, the Johnsons, must be Brits."

"Not American?"

"I doubt it. The husband's first name is Jocelyn, and you don't get too many of those in the States. So there's no language problem there — Elena can do the same pitch she did with Madame Castellaci. But we can't count on the Rimbauds speaking

English, so I'm wondering if we might recruit Mimi for the job. Can she be charming and persuasive over the phone?"

"Are you kidding? She proposed to me over the phone. One day I'll tell you about it."

"Great. Elena can give her a little coaching on the sales pitch, and then all we have to do is work on the dates. How's the head?"

"Almost back to normal. All I need now is a beer."

Using the phone numbers listed in the police reports, Mimi and Elena made their calls, and reported back to Sam and Philippe.

Mimi's conversation with Monsieur Rimbaud had started in an atmosphere of suspicion — quite normal with the rich French, so Mimi said — but had improved as soon as the possibility of reduced insurance premiums was mentioned. He also admitted, when Mimi asked him, that he spoke good English; certainly good enough, as he said, for an American insurance inspector. Mimi's verdict was that he was a snob with a sense of humor. A date was fixed for the following week.

Elena's call had also been productive. Mr. Johnson was indeed an Englishman, affable and with the plummy drawl of the English upper class, an accent that had reminded Elena of a character from *Downton Abbey.* His enthusiasm for the idea of a photographer taking pictures of his home had surprised her. She had anticipated a possible problem there, but not a bit of it. The run of the house, he had promised her, and the garden as well, if that's what the photographer needed. Once again, a date was fixed for the following week.

"So it looks like a busy couple of days," said Sam. "But I have an idea. We'll be in Monaco on Tuesday, Antibes on Wednesday, and I think we deserve a little rest and relaxation in between. How do you feel about us spending Tuesday night in Antibes, instead of coming back to Marseille? They tell me there are one or two decent hotels there."

"Well," said Philippe, "there's the Hôtel du Cap, of course."

"Now you're talking," said Elena. "Ever since Francis told me about that place I've wanted to stay there."

"Me too," said Mimi.

Sam looked at Philippe, and grinned. "I guess that's a yes."

Lunch at the Fitzgerald house on Cap Ferrat had gone well. The houseguests had been charmed by Coco and her father, and the all-American menu of barbecued ribs and key lime pie had been tempting enough to make the ladies abandon their diets. It was a well-fed and satisfied group that lingered on the terrace over a final cup of coffee before answering the call of the siesta.

During lunch, there had been a great deal of talk about Saint-Tropez. None of them, neither the Fitzgeralds nor their guests, had actually been there. Coco had been astonished, and had suggested that a visit to this mythical spot was an essential part of the South of France experience. "It has a great atmosphere, the people have to be seen to be believed, and it's a lot of fun," said Coco. In fact, she could recommend one of her favorite hotels: La Résidence de la Pinède, right on the Gulf of Saint-Tropez, with its own private beach and a Michelin three-star restaurant. The manager, she said, was a great friend of hers.

This had solved a problem for the houseguests. That very morning, around the pool, they had been discussing how they could repay the Fitzgeralds for their kind and generous hospitality, and what better gift could there be? Why not take them off to Saint-Tropez for the weekend, and stay in this idyllic hotel?

That evening over drinks, the Hoffmans, the Dillons, and the Greenbergs had presented their idea to the Fitzgeralds. Kathy and Fitz were delighted, and so, amid much hugging and kissing, it was decided. The weekend after the party, they would all be off to the delights of Saint-Tropez.

"The trouble with Monaco," said Philippe, "is that they've put up so many high-rise buildings there isn't anywhere you can legally park the car." He pulled into a space that was clearly marked "For Residents Only." "This will have to do." He reached under his seat, pulled out a stethoscope and a folder with the name Docteur Chevalier prominently displayed on the cover, and placed them carefully on top of the dashboard above the steering wheel.

"Who's Doctor Chevalier?" asked Sam.

"It's my *nom de parking.* You'd be amazed how often it works."

The Rimbauds' house was in the old town, not far from the royal palace. A narrow, almost modest building, it was worth, according to Philippe, double-digit millions. The view of the Mediterranean helped, of course, but it was Monaco's tax structure, so much less demanding than in neighboring France, that made it such a popular home for millionaires, including tennis professionals, yacht owners, and shady businessmen.

Monsieur Rimbaud himself came to the door to let them in. A tall, slim man in his sixties, he had the kind of face one often sees in France: high cheekbones, prominent nose, and a mouth with stern, unsmiling lips. He led them into his study and indicated the two chairs in front of his desk.

He glanced at the business card Sam had given him. "Very well, Monsieur Levitt. What can I do for you?"

"I hope it's what *we* can do for *you,*" said Sam, and began his pitch.

Rimbaud let Sam finish before speaking. "This is all very interesting. Unfortunately, it comes too late to bring back my wife's jewels." He shrugged and managed a half smile. "Life is like that sometimes, don't you think — so inconvenient."

"If you'll allow us to have a brief look around the house I think we can help you ensure that this particular inconvenience doesn't happen again."

Rimbaud nodded. "Very well." He looked at Philippe. "I see that your colleague has a camera. I assume that this is for reference purposes, but I do not want photographs of this house circulated. Privacy is a vanishing luxury these days, and we value what little we have. Is that clear?"

"I couldn't agree more," said Sam, hoping that Philippe was able to conceal his disappointment. Chez Rimbaud was certainly not going to feature in his series on houses of the rich and famous. "And you're quite right. We just need a few anonymous reference shots of your security arrangements for our technicians back in the States."

With some reluctance, Rimbaud agreed. He shadowed Philippe around the house, pointing out the alarm devices and showing the wall safe, which was, as usual, hidden behind a large painting. Within half an hour it was over, and Philippe and Sam had settled in the nearest café.

"Nice house," said Philippe. "Very elegant. Pity I can't use it."

"You know what struck me? He didn't seem at all upset by the robbery. When he mentioned it, he might have been talking about some minor domestic hiccup. No emotion, not like the Castellacis."

Philippe dipped a sugar lump into his coffee and popped it into his mouth. "That might just be an act. I mean, suppose he'd lifted the jewels himself. It might look a little suspicious if he had an attack of hysterics every time the subject came up."

"Do you think he did it himself?"

"You saw the house. It's like a fortress. It's in the middle of Monaco, where the police nearly outnumber the residents. You couldn't even have a private *pipi* here without being caught on camera. So if I had to bet on it, I'd certainly say it was an inside job. No wonder he wants to protect his privacy."

Their day took a turn for the better when they reached the Hôtel du Cap in the late afternoon. At Elena's urging, they had decided to share a two-bedroom suite that had its own Jacuzzi on the private terrace. And there they were, Elena and Mimi, soaking away the aftereffects of a taxing few hours in the hotel spa.

"How was it?" asked Elena.

Sam and Philippe shrugged in unison.

"Oh. That bad. Never mind — there's always tomorrow. And you've made two girls blissfully happy."

"Then our lives have not been lived in vain. Come on, Philippe, let's get undressed and join the ladies."

CHAPTER 18

The four friends began their day with what Elena called a bathrobe breakfast, taken on the terrace. The sun was pleasantly warm, the sky a fine early-morning blue, the sea shimmered, and all was well with the world.

Elena stretched, tilting her head up to the sun. "It's going to be tough getting back to real life."

"Don't worry," said Philippe, "there isn't much real life around here, and certainly not where we're going. The west side of Cap d'Antibes, where the Johnsons live, is, if you believe the real estate agents, the best place to be. You'd be lucky to find a decent little house here for less than five or six million." He grinned. "Not that I want to make you feel poor, Sam."

"Too late," said Sam. "I had them send our bill up with breakfast."

But, as they all agreed, it was money well spent. They felt refreshed and pampered, filled with a sense of well-being and the optimism that so often comes with it. Surely today would produce a breakthrough in the investigation.

Mimi and Elena decided to leave the men to it and spend the morning exploring the streets of Antibes, "the only town on the coast that has kept its soul," according to Graham Greene. Sam and Philippe, their pitch at the ready, made their way through the narrow, quiet roads of the Cap until they came to the double wrought-iron gates that led up the drive to a sprawling, cream-colored house. Philippe pressed the intercom buzzer, to be greeted by Johnson's voice.

"You're the insurance chappies, yes? Bang on time. Mind the dog on your way up the drive. He's English, so he rather likes biting French cars."

The gates swung open. Philippe started up the drive, but braked at the sight of a king-sized Rhodesian ridgeback who had emerged from a clump of bushes and was watching them closely from the side of the drive. Was that a smile or a snarl?

"Are you any good with dogs?" asked Philippe.

"Labradors and cocker spaniels. Nothing like this. I'd go very slowly."

Yard by cautious yard the car continued up the drive, escorted by the dog, and it was with considerable relief that they saw there was someone waiting for them outside the front door. It was Jocelyn Johnson himself, a fair-haired, thickset man with a brick-red face and a broad, welcoming smile. "Don't get out until I get the dog in. Percy! Come!" With some reluctance, Percy allowed himself to be chivvied into a large kennel at one end of the porch: Sam and Philippe got out of the car and followed Johnson through the house and onto the terrace, with its millionaire's view. A woman wearing a straw hat and gardening gloves came over from a thicket of red roses to greet them.

"My wife, Angie," said Johnson. "She's responsible for all this."

He waved an arm at the immaculate garden. "A local chap comes in for the heavy stuff, of course, but the roses are all her own work — isn't that right, sweetie?"

Angie smiled as she took off her gloves and put her pruning shears on the table before shaking hands with Sam and Philippe. "Someone's got to do it, and I'm afraid poor JJ isn't qualified. I sometimes wonder if he knows the difference between a rose and a nettle. Now, would you all like coffee? I'll ask Sabine to bring it out."

"What a lovely place you have here," said Sam. "So peaceful — the robbery must have been a terrible shock."

"It was. In fact, that's why we brought Percy over from our place in Hampshire. If he'd been on duty here, the burglar would have been in shreds."

"Well, let's try to make sure it never happens again."

By now they were settled around the table, and Sabine was fussing with coffee cups and a plate of chocolate digestive biscuits. "My little weakness," Jocelyn said. "Now then. Before you get down to business, I feel I ought to come clean. This wretched robbery has really affected Angie very badly. She just doesn't feel comfortable here anymore, which I can understand." He sighed. "Anyway, cut a long story short, we've decided to sell the house and find something more secure in Monaco. So I'm awfully sorry, but I think we've wasted your time."

"Don't worry," said Sam, "I absolutely understand. But if we could take a look around the house, it would help the report I'm putting together for our people in the States."

"Of course," said Johnson, who seemed

relieved to be able to offer this small consolation. He took them inside for a guided
tour.

It was while they were in the library that
Johnson stepped away from them to take a
phone call.

"Sam, I've had a thought." Philippe's
voice was low and conspiratorial. "This
house is beautiful — a terrific subject for
the magazine, and a friendly piece might
help him sell it. What do you think?"

Sam looked over at Johnson, still deep in
conversation. "I think he'd like that. Why
not ask him?"

"He *loved* the idea," a jubilant Philippe said
as they drove away from the house, making
a careful detour to avoid Percy, who had
escaped his kennel and was lurking on the
drive. "He's going to call me as soon as he's
checked it out with 'she who must be
obeyed' — I guess that's his wife — and
then we'll fix a date for Mimi and me to go
back for an all-day shoot. How about that?"

"I think you've had more luck than I had.
This place is just like the other two —
stuffed with security gadgets, and a safe that
looks like something out of a bank vault."

"Well, at least we tried." Philippe glanced
at his friend. "Don't get depressed. It was

always a long shot."

When Sam and Elena arrived back at Le Pharo, they found that Reboul's *petite amie,* Monica Chung, had just arrived from Hong Kong, and Reboul was full of plans for outings and adventures — Corsica, the Côte d'Azur, the Casino at Monte Carlo (like most Chinese, she loved to gamble), maybe even a weekend or two in Paris. Elena and Sam had never seen him in such high spirits, and it was contagious, putting an end to Sam's lingering sense of anticlimax.

"Are we going to be allowed to see her?" asked Elena. "Or are you keeping her to yourself?"

"Before she comes down, tell me, how was today? Clues? Breakthroughs? Any mysteries solved?"

"I wish," said Sam. "But it was more like a dead end, case closed. Same as the other two. Maybe I should drop the whole thing, and take up golf."

Elena rolled her eyes. "I don't think I could stand the excitement."

Further discussion of Sam's future plans was interrupted by the arrival of Monica, dressed for the occasion in a cream silk cheongsam. As Elena and Sam remembered from their first meeting a couple of years earlier, she was a remarkably beautiful woman, almost a miniature, with delicate features and shining black hair. It was hard to imagine her as one of Hong Kong's toughest businesswomen. The sight of her reminded Elena and Sam of the evening, some time ago, when Reboul had told them about the new love of his life.

Monica was the last in line of the Hong Kong Chungs. Her father, known in the local business world as King Chung, doted on his daughter, spoiled her shamelessly, and was determined that she would one day take over the running of the Chung empire. As part of her introduction to the world outside Hong Kong he had sent her, at the age of twenty, to Europe.

She had been amused by London, despite the weather, and impressed by Rome. But when she arrived in Paris, she was hooked — by its beauty, by its ambience, and, most of all, by some of its masculine inhabitants. Unfortunately for her father's hopes of marrying her off to a pillar of Hong Kong society, she had discovered Frenchmen. Their charm, their elegance, those tantalizing whiffs of expensive aftershave — she loved it all. Her quick trip to Paris turned into a six-month stay, and by the time she stepped off the plane at Hong Kong International, her accompanied baggage included a fiancé, Jean-Luc Descartes, a graduate of the École Nationale d'Administration, with a promising future in French politics.

It was a relationship, as Monica's father had quickly pointed out, with a fundamental problem: Jean-Luc's future was in Paris; Monica's was in Hong Kong. There followed an uneasy period of trial — romantic reunions in Paris or Hong Kong followed by returns to real life. It couldn't work, and it didn't. The periods apart became longer. Jean-Luc met someone in Paris, Monica met someone in Hong Kong, and eventually each of them married. Jean-Luc was now the father of three children, and Monica was now a divorced woman dedicated to her numerous companies. And then she met Francis Reboul, who was on a business trip to Hong Kong. Her fondness for Frenchmen, dormant for many years, resurfaced and bloomed, and they were now working out a way of spending more and more time together.

Monica was smiling as she went up to Elena and Sam. "Lovely to see you again. And now Francis tells me you're going to be our new neighbors. That's wonderful. Perhaps you can keep him out of trouble with all those Marseille ladies."

"Francis," said Elena, "you're blushing."

"I always blush when I'm thirsty. Champagne, anyone?"

"I'm not sure," said Sam. "Have we finished the Chinese *rosé*?"

Philippe's call came through as Elena and Sam were getting ready for bed. "It's all set," he said, "and so we're going over next week. Johnson said his wife thought it sounded like a jolly good wheeze." There was a thoughtful pause. "Tell me something, Sam. You've met more English people than I have. They all say that English is a global language, but they seem to use a special dialect. I mean, what is this good wheeze? And why is it jolly? *Ils sont bizarres, les anglais.*"

"They certainly are. I think it must be the English climate. It does peculiar things to people. Have you ever watched cricket? Very strange."

Kathy Fitzgerald put down the phone and punched the air in triumph before going in search of her husband. She found him with Frank Dillon in the living room, where they were sipping their Scotch, smoking their cigars, watching CNN, and bemoaning the state of the world.

"Fitz! Good news!"

"Go tell CNN, sweetheart. They need it."

"No, seriously — Coco just called, and she's managed to get us all into that hotel on the beach at Saint-Tropez. The manager's a friend of hers, so she persuaded him to move a few people around to make room for us. Isn't that great?"

Fitz smiled at his wife's enthusiasm. This vacation was turning out pretty well, he thought. The houseguests were all happy to go off in the morning, coming back in the evening in time for a drink before dinner. Such a welcome change from last year's guests, who had hung around the house all the time, waiting to be entertained. He had come to dread what he called the early-morning inquisition — "What are we going to do today?" — as if he were the entertainment director of a resort camp. This year, thank God, was different. Even so, an excursion to Saint-Tropez would make a very pleasant break.

He patted the seat next to him, and Kathy joined him on the couch, kissing his forehead as she sat down. It did him good to see her so happy.

CHAPTER 19

Sam, who was prone to the occasional twinge of guilt after eating too much and exercising too little, had begun to run every day. His attempts to interest Elena in joining him having been loudly dismissed, he had recruited as a running companion Nemo, the chef's dog, the only gourmet mongrel in Provence. In the morning, the two of them would set off along the narrow footpath that led to Elena and Sam's house, with Nemo bounding ahead and Sam doing his best to bound behind him.

Despite the early hour — usually between 7:30 and 8:30 — there were always workers on site already hard at it, banging, drilling, sawing, cursing, and whistling. And there was always Claude, the *chef de chantier,* to point out all the latest marvels that he and his team had accomplished since Sam's last visit, which had been all of twenty-four hours before.

Reboul, every time Sam updated him, had been amazed by the speed of progress. "Where do these guys think they are? This is Provence, for heaven's sake. If they keep up this pace, they'll ruin the region's reputation."

It was true that the work had so far gone unusually smoothly: terraces had been laid around the house, doors and windows installed, kitchen and bathrooms almost there, and floors refinished. It wouldn't be long before the painters moved in. Meanwhile, Elena was racing around furniture stores like a woman possessed.

Sam and Nemo were at the house catching their breath when Philippe called. He and Mimi were setting off for Cap d'Antibes to spend the day taking photographs of the Johnson house. "Just wanted to check with you," he said. "Is there anything you specially want us to cover?"

"I can't think of anything I didn't see when we had a look around the other day. Just concentrate on getting the stuff for your piece."

"*D'accord.* What are you doing today?"

"Improving my Provençal education. Francis wants to introduce Monica to *boules,* and so we're all going to watch a game in Marseille this evening. Will that be fun?"

"You tell me after you've watched the game."

After a swim, Sam felt strong enough for a much-delayed discussion with Elena about furniture, and the rest of the morning passed in a blur of fabric swatches and pages clipped from magazines. Sam's decorative instincts ran to muted tones and strict simplicity; Elena had a fondness for brighter colors and picturesque clutter. In the end, they agreed to ask Coco to act as referee.

Over at the house on Cap d'Antibes, the shoot was going well. Mrs. Johnson, after welcoming Mimi and Philippe, had disappeared into the garden, fully armed with her pruning shears and several sprays to counter everything from greenfly to the gluttonous caterpillar. JJ was left in charge, which was clearly his favorite position. He had assumed the dual responsibilities of client and art director, pointing out possible subjects for Mimi to photograph while emphasizing to Philippe the merits of various paintings and pieces of furniture and the high standard of workmanship throughout. He was also at pains to show them both the extensive security installations, including the safe in his library. It was hidden behind a range of bookshelves that swung open at the touch of a concealed button, although, for obvious reasons, this was not to be photographed.

In every way it was an impressive house, and Philippe hardly stopped taking notes. By the end of the morning, Mimi was satisfied that she had finished with the interior; in the afternoon, she wanted to cover the garden — especially those glorious roses — the pool, and the views. By the time they sat down to lunch on the terrace, there was a general feeling that it had been a most productive morning.

Lunch, which JJ had described as "a bit of a picnic," turned out to be stuffed courgette flowers, lobster, a cheese board fit for a three-star restaurant, and chocolate mousse. Philippe had some difficulty resisting the wines, which started with Chassagne-Montrachet and ended with a '91 Château d'Yquem, and Johnson's example didn't help. His thirst was spectacular — "going through the wine list," as he said — and the more he drank the more he talked, mostly about himself and his brilliant career in London's stock exchange. Angie, his wife, had obviously heard it all before, and left after the lobster to attend to pressing business in the garden.

Mimi was the next to escape, saying that she had to catch the afternoon light, leaving Philippe smiling and nodding at JJ's exploits. But eventually the wine did its work, and JJ went off, much to Philippe's relief, for what he called "a little shuteye."

Philippe found Mimi perched in a tree, her camera lens scanning the views. She peered at him through the leaves. "Is it safe to come down, or is he still talking?"

"He went off for a nap. How's it going?"

"Just about done. I think I've got some good stuff — everywhere you look is like an Impressionist painting. Should make a great piece." Mimi changed lenses. "One last shot of the pool, now that the light's softer, and that's it."

Ten minutes later, they went in search of Angie to make their goodbyes, and to offer their thanks and apologies for having taken so long. "But it will be worth it," said Mimi. "You'll see when we send you the photographs."

"What do you think I should wear for a *boules* match?" Elena had just come out of the shower, and had a towel wrapped round her.

Sam studied her for a moment. "What you've got on looks pretty good. Maybe a hat, just to finish it off?"

Elena went to the dressing room, shaking her head.

Le Cochonnet, more of an institution than a mere bar, is in the western suburbs of Marseille, far from the elegant boutiques and restaurants of the city center. It is not a place for those who consider *boules* as nothing more than an amusing way to pass an afternoon. Here it is played by men with an addiction to the game, *les hommes sérieux.* Passions run high. Money has been known to change hands. Amateurs are advised to watch, but not to play. This introduction was passed on to the others by Reboul during the drive over from Le Pharo; he also gave them a brief guide to the rules of the game.

In theory, he told them, it's very simple. There is a small wooden ball, the *but,* or *cochonnet,* that is thrown from one end of the court to the other, a distance of about twelve meters. The first player — there can be one, two, or three on each side — then tries to throw his *boule* to land as close as possible to the *but.* His opponents will do their best to remove it, either by a direct hit

185

along the ground, or by bombing from above. Where matters get complicated is when players go to measure the distance of their *boules* from the *but*. The closer the throw is to the target ball the better, which you might think is an easy judgment to make. But no. Measurements, usually in millimeters, are hotly disputed. Fingers are wagged, arms are waved, accusations of impaired vision fly back and forth. Measuring gadgets are produced and brandished like weapons. To the observer, it looks as though physical violence is imminent. And yet, ten minutes later, there are the opponents, laughing over their drinks, the best of friends once again.

"In other words," said Reboul, "it's a typically French mixture — drama, posturing, threats, denials, and a drink to finish things off."

"Sounds just like Congress back in Washington," said Sam. "Especially the posturing."

They joined a long line of cars parked under a row of plane trees overlooking the *boulodrome,* a large expanse of *clapicette.* This is hard-packed, sandy gravel, smooth enough to let the *boule* run, with just enough bounce and surface irregularity to cause some interesting diversions from the straight line. There was enough space for three courts, all of them busy, and noisy: argument, groans at a misplaced throw, grunts of triumph — and punctuating it all, the metallic clack of *boule* hitting *boule.*

Monica was fascinated. "Well, it doesn't look too difficult," she said. "I think I could play this."

"Me too," said Elena. "Looks like fun."

"Ah," said Reboul, "anyone can play *boules* — that's one of its charms. But not everyone can play well. You watch these players. They're twelve meters away from their target, but they'll hit it nine times out of ten. Now, come with me. I want to introduce you to some very important basic equipment."

He led the way into the bar, where they were inspected, first by a group of old men playing cards at a table by the door, and then by two players standing at the bar resting between matches, their *boules* beside them on the zinc surface. The room was long and low-ceilinged, dominated by a wall of bottles. A cat snoozed on top of an old and dusty television, which was tuned to a replay of an Olympique de Marseille soccer match.

At the bar, Reboul held up four fingers to

the barman, who was obviously used to the signal.

He raised an eyebrow. *"Pastaga?"*

Reboul nodded. *"Pastaga."*

The barman set out four glasses, and poured into each one a generous shot of dark, transparent yellow liquid. He placed ice cubes and a jug of water next to the glasses, and stood back, arms folded, to watch. It was rare to see such elegant women taking this particular drink, and he was interested in their reaction.

Reboul busied himself adding water and ice, and the drinks changed color, from dark yellow to a softer shade, pale and milky. *"Voilà,"* he said, distributing the glasses, "mother's milk for every *boules* player."

Monica held her glass up to her nose, and sniffed. "Aniseed?"

"Pastis," said Reboul. "Aniseed, with herbs and a little licorice root. Delicious, but be careful — it's forty-five percent alcohol."

Monica and Elena took their first taste, and then another. They approved, raising their glasses to the barman. He smiled and nodded. These people were obviously *sympathique.* Reaching to a shelf behind him, he took down a small statuette and placed it on the bar, in front of Reboul. It was made from pottery, and showed a young

188

woman in a low-cut red dress, leaning against a tall placard marked "13 à o Fanny."

Reboul was grinning. "This is Fanny, a famous barmaid many years ago, and a keen student of *boules*. Now, the game is won by the first player to reach thirteen points. If his opponent fails to score a single point, he has to pay a penalty, and this is where Fanny comes in." Reboul turned the statuette around, to show that Fanny had pulled her dress up to her waist, revealing a fine pair of naked buttocks. "And there is the penalty: The loser has to kiss Fanny's — how shall I put it?"

"Fanny?" said Monica.

"Exactly, my dear. Apparently, there really was a barmaid named Fanny, who was very much appreciated by the local players."

They took their drinks outside and stopped to watch as one player, tossing a *boule* from hand to hand, took up his position and studied the group of balls clustered around the *but*. He crouched, his eyes fixed on his target. Slowly, his throwing arm went backwards, paused, and quickly came forward to release the *boule* in a high, graceful arc that landed among the other *boules* with a multiple clack, scattering them across the court.

"This game is vicious," said Sam. "Maybe even worse than croquet."

On the court, the players had gathered around the winning *boule,* either to celebrate or to start a litany of outraged disputes and arm-waving that looked set to continue all evening.

"This will go on until they get thirsty," said Reboul. "But you get the idea. It's not the quietest of games."

Elena finished her drink. "I love it," she said. "All of it. Sam, we could have a court at the house. But why aren't there any women playing?"

"Who knows?" said Sam. "Maybe they're getting ready to console the losers."

CHAPTER 20

"These are very good," said Philippe. "The magazine's going to love them."

He and Mimi were going through the photographs she had taken of the Johnson house, and they were extremely inviting. The rooms looked spacious and elegant, the terraces shady and cool, and the views were spectacular.

"Did he tell you how much they want when they sell it?" asked Mimi.

"Not exactly, although he did mutter at one point about eight or ten million. Whether that was a fair guess or a mixture of booze and optimism is hard to say. But houses around here are certainly not bargains."

Mimi had stopped at one of the interior shots, and had bent closer to the screen for another look. "That's odd," she said. "I hadn't really noticed it at the time. Look." She tilted the computer so that Philippe had a clearer view. It was a handsome image showing Johnson's large, leather-topped desk, furnished with the various trimmings — silver letter-opener, Lalique owl paper-weight, red *Economist* desk diary, mahogany in-tray — of a prosperous executive's office. But Mimi's finger was pointing lower down, at the bottom of the photograph, which showed the main desk drawer. The handle was bronze, in the shape of a woman's hand, hinged at the wrist.

Mimi was frowning and shaking her head. "I'm sure I've seen that before, but I can't think where."

"Don't worry. It'll come to you. Let's go back to the exteriors."

They continued to go through the shots, picking out the best for the article. Once they had agreed on the selection, they sent one set of photographs to the Johnsons for their approval; a second set went to Claudine, the features editor of *Salut!,* at the magazine's Nice office.

With the day's work done, they went off to meet Elena and Sam at their house. Mimi had never seen it, but she had liked Philippe's idea of having their wedding party there, and this evening they were going to work out some of the details.

They arrived at the house to be greeted

by a buzz of activity, with the sounds of workmen in full cry coming through the open front door. Inside, having sidestepped a thoughtful electrician scratching his head as he brooded over a spaghetti of wiring, they found Elena and Sam hunched in front of a set of plans in what would shortly be a fully fitted kitchen.

"Thank the Lord you're here," said Sam. "I got completely lost somewhere between ceramic hobs and steam ovens. My kitchen experience is pretty much limited to toasters and frying pans."

"This will help," said Philippe. He hoisted onto the table a large freezer bag. Inside were two bottles of chilled *rosé,* four glasses, and a corkscrew.

"I think you've saved Sam's life," said Elena. "I was about to throw him off the cliff. Why is it that men get so grouchy about kitchens?"

With their glasses filled, Elena took them on a guided tour, suggesting possible spots for drinks, a buffet supper, and dancing. Mimi was thrilled with it all, especially the terraces that went around three sides of the house. For the party, Elena had planned to put up white canvas awnings to provide shade from the sun or shelter from, God forbid, any rain.

Mimi was also most impressed by the standard of finish and the attention to detail inside the house, and Elena was quick to give credit where it was due.

"It's Coco," she said. "She's been amazing — never forgets anything, keeps every last detail in one of her little notebooks. The workmen would do anything for her and, of course, she speaks perfect English. What a lucky find. She even bought us a housewarming gift. Come and take a look." They stopped outside the front door, and Elena demonstrated the knocker. "She thinks it might be eighteenth-century, and it really works with the door."

Mimi took a close look. It was exactly the same — even down to the shape of the woman's hand — as the handle on Johnson's desk drawer. Larger, obviously, but the similarity was unmistakable. "It's beautiful. So is the door. It's going to be a lovely house."

Mimi didn't mention it again until they were in the car. "It's starting to bother me," she said. "I know I've seen that hand somewhere else, not just the Johnson house."

"Another knocker?"

"No — I'm sure it was a miniature."

Later that evening, they were celebrating a rare night away from *les people* by going

194

to bed early and watching an old Truffaut movie on television. As one poignant moment was following another, Philippe abruptly got up and went to his office, coming back with his laptop. "I just remembered something. The photographs I took at the Castellaci house."

"Is this going to be more exciting than Truffaut?"

"Could be." He opened the Castellaci file and began clicking through the photographs. "*Et voilà!* That's where you've seen it. Take a look." He passed the laptop across to Mimi. And there, partly obscured by shadow, was the door of a closet in Madame Castellaci's dressing room. The closet handle was a miniature bronze female hand, hinged at the wrist.

"We need to make a couple of calls," said Philippe. "It's too late now; we'll make them in the morning." The final moments of Truffaut passed by unwatched.

Was it coincidence? A new decorative fad? Mimi and Philippe were still discussing it over breakfast the following morning, an impatient Philippe repeatedly consulting his watch until he felt he could make his calls. And then Mimi's phone rang.

It was Claudine, and she was extravagantly

pleased. "Sweetie! I'm thrilled! The photos are divine! So perfect for *Salut!*" And on she went, every sentence an exclamation of joy, culminating with an invitation for them both to come to Nice right away, where they could go over a few details before a celebration lunch.

Needless to say, Mimi was flattered and excited. Philippe had shaved in honor of the occasion, and it was a happy two-hour drive that brought them to Claudine's office, situated — *naturellement* — on the Promenade des Anglais, where Claudine herself was waiting to greet them. She was, as one would expect from a woman working on the fringes of fashion and celebrity, relentlessly chic — the latest *coiffure,* this season's perky summer dress, and the most avant-garde shoes. She admitted to being thirty-nine, that wonderfully elastic age, and she was determined to stay thirty-nine for several years to come.

"So," she said, taking both of Mimi's hands in hers, "at last I meet the genius behind the lens! Come and have a glass of Champagne." She led them into her office, a shrine to celebrity, with photographs of *les people* lining the walls.

The Champagne was poured, the toasts were made, and then the photographs, which had been printed up and pinned to the wall, were inspected and gushed over. It was Philippe who interrupted by mentioning that the owners had decided to sell. There was a sudden silence before Claudine, scenting an exclusive, suggested that *Salut!* could break the news that this magnificent property was for sale. That is, if the owners agreed. She looked at Philippe, eyebrows raised. He took the hint and took out his phone.

"Mr. Johnson, it's Philippe Davin. I hope I'm not disturbing you?"

"Not at all, dear boy, not at all. In fact, I was going to call you to say how much we like the snaps. Couldn't have done better myself — they should put another million on the price."

"I'm delighted you're pleased. Mr. Johnson, I'm in a meeting at the moment with the magazine's editor, and she's had a very good idea — an exclusive that would include the information that the house is for sale. In effect, it would be like a six-page ad."

Johnson hardly hesitated. "Splendid idea," he said. "Tell your editor to get in touch with me — there'll probably be some paperwork to sort out. You can't blow your nose here in France without an official piece of paper."

"One last thing," said Philippe. "The magazine would like to give the decorator a mention, if that's OK with you."

"By all means. Lovely gal, perfect English, Coco something."

"Dumas?"

"That's it. Coco Dumas."

Claudine was so pleased with the call that she almost forgot to check her makeup before they left the office to go to a nearby restaurant. As Mimi said later, it was like having lunch with royalty. The headwaiter fawned over Claudine, the chef came out of his kitchen to give her his personal recommendations, and the *sommelier* came to the table cradling a bottle of her favorite wine.

"It looks like they know you here," said Philippe to Claudine.

"It's our little canteen," she said. "So close to the office, and they're all so sweet."

And, somewhat to Philippe's surprise, the canteen cuisine was excellent: simple, fresh, and tasty. It would have been even better with a glass or two of wine, but as he was driving, and as the *autoroute* was crawling with gendarmes, he had to settle for San Pellegrino.

During the drive back to Marseille, Philippe asked Mimi to make two calls — the first to

Madame Castellaci, the second to Monsieur Rimbaud in Monaco. They confirmed what Philippe had now begun to feel was more than just a hunch, and after checking that Elena and Sam would be there, they made their way straight to Le Pharo.

"What's the panic?" said Sam as he met them on the terrace.

"Thirst," said Philippe. "Where are you hiding the *rosé*?"

They settled at a table, with a fine view of the dipping sun, and Philippe delivered his news. "Those three houses that were robbed so professionally? We just found out who renovated them all: Coco Dumas."

Elena was frowning. "So? She must have done dozens of houses along the coast."

"Look — I know that she's your new best friend, but you have to admit that it's an amazing coincidence. Sam, what do you think?"

"Well, her name didn't appear on any of the police reports. But then, why would it? Police generally aren't too interested in interior decorators." He took a thoughtful sip of wine. "And when you think about it, someone in her position couldn't be better placed to get into a house. As we know from working with her, she takes care of every-thing, all the details, from the kitchen drawers to the alarm system. She would know all the codes, because she probably helped to set them. She could easily keep a duplicate set of keys, without the owner knowing. So yes, it's technically possible that she had something to do with the robberies."

Elena wasn't at all convinced. "I think that's ridiculous. She has a great business. Why risk it?"

"Money," said Sam. "You've seen the figures. The total stolen from those three houses adds up to about twelve million euros, tax free. Not bad for a sideline. Don't get me wrong — I like Coco, and she's doing a fine job for us, but these are practically risk-free robberies for someone in her situation."

"OK, Mr. Smartass, so what are you going to do? Call her up and say, Gotcha?"

"I don't know." Sam shrugged his shoulders. "I really don't know. Anyone got any ideas?"

CHAPTER 21

It was a perplexed and thoughtful Sam that Reboul found on the terrace that evening — although not too thoughtful to notice that his host was wearing a beautifully cut dinner jacket.

"Ah, Francis. You shouldn't have dressed up for me."

Reboul grinned, and stroked the silk lapel of his jacket. "What do you think? Monica had it made for me in Hong Kong, and I'm christening it tonight. We're going to the opera. Did you know that Marseille has a wonderful opera house? The original one was built in the seventeenth century, on a tennis court. Anyway, tonight it's *La Traviata.*" He paused to look more closely at Sam. "You seem very quiet. Are you alright?"

"My friend, you're not going to like this, but I have to tell you something." Sam sighed, and stared down at his drink. "I'm beginning to think that Coco Dumas was in some way connected with these unsolved robberies."

After a long silence, it was Reboul's turn to sigh. "I'm sorry to say it wouldn't surprise me. Money for her is an addiction. But tell me, what makes you think she was involved?"

Sam went through it all, starting with the accidental discovery of the miniature hands and moving on to the confirmation by the three different robbery victims that Coco had renovated all three houses. "It's all too much of a coincidence."

Reboul shook his head, and poured himself some more wine. "As I've told you, Coco and I have a history, and I think I know her well. One of the reasons the relationship ended was her obsession with money. When she realized it wasn't going to come from marrying me is when it all started to fall apart. So the idea of making millions from stealing her clients' diamonds without too much risk could easily have appealed to her. Also, I happen to know that her father, whom I met a couple of times, has some kind of business in Antwerp, which is where diamonds often go for a change of identity. So that might have been an added attraction." He looked over Sam's

shoulder, and stood up. "How delightful —
here's Madame Butterfly."

It was a smiling, elegant Monica, in a
floor-length dress of her favorite cream silk.

"You're a lucky man," said Sam.

"I am indeed," said Reboul, looking at his
watch. "But I'm also a late man. We have to
go. Sam, let's have breakfast together tomorrow and we can talk some more."

When Sam found Elena, she was in the
kitchen of Le Pharo, paying close attention
to Alphonse, who was explaining the finer
points of cooking with a steam oven.

"Sam, we must have one of these steam
ovens. Simple, healthy, no grease — they're
great."

Sam nodded wisely, and settled down to
wait for the end of the lesson. He was still
trying to get used to the idea of Elena as a
kitchen goddess. As far as he knew, she had
rarely attempted anything more ambitious
than a salami sandwich when she was
obliged to eat at home. This was a promising development.

They said goodnight to Alphonse and
went back to the terrace, where Sam
brought Elena up to date on his conversation with Reboul. "What really amazed me
was that he didn't seem shocked, or even

very surprised. And he must know her better than anyone."

Elena had hardly stopped shaking her head since Sam had started talking. "Sam, I'm sorry, but I really don't believe it. Why are you so obsessed with this, anyway?"

"Look, there's no such thing as a perfect crime, and this is beyond coincidence. So let's just say it's professional curiosity. Indulge me, OK? Come on — let's go to Chez Marcel for dinner."

"Promise not to spend the evening talking about it?"

"Promise. It's your turn. My whole being longs to know more about steam ovens."

They arrived at the restaurant, and were surprised to find Mimi and Philippe already at a table in the corner, looking unusually glamorous: Mimi in a classic little black dress, and Philippe in a dinner jacket.

"Where's my camera?" said Sam. "Look at you both. Don't tell me — you're going to the opera."

Philippe grimaced. "I wish we were, but we're covering a gala evening at the Sofitel. And you won't believe this: our dear client told us that he didn't want us to take any photographs of his guests eating — maybe they drool or something — so he suggested that we eat in the hotel kitchen, and come out after dinner. To hell with that. But tell me, how's the investigation going? Found any clues? Oh, I forgot to tell you: Coco Dumas will be at the Fitzgerald party next week."

Sam thought he heard a suppressed groan coming from Elena, but before he could take the subject any further, Mimi dragged Philippe away to the delights of the gala evening.

Elena was not looking happy when they sat down. "I thought you promised not to talk about it?"

"I didn't. Not a word. I was just answering Philippe's question."

But Elena's face remained unsmiling. "Don't stay mad," said Sam. "It's bad for the complexion. Now, I have two secret weapons to cheer you up: First, we will talk about nothing except our dream kitchen. We will leave no stove unturned. We might even think about a kitchen-warming party. And second, I see that tonight there is *panna cotta* on the menu, with your favorite caramel topping. Do I see the beginnings of a smile?"

He did indeed, and the rest of dinner went according to plan: The kitchen was exhaustively discussed. Decisions were made by Elena, and endorsed by Sam, even though once or twice he wasn't too sure of what he was endorsing. Smiles reappeared. Warm words were exchanged. By the time they left the restaurant, Sam felt he had regained considerable credit in the Elena Morales bank.

It was one of those early-summer evenings when the air had an almost tangible softness and the stars an extra brilliance. As Elena said, it was too beautiful to go to bed, so they strolled around the Vieux Port until they came to a Corsican café, one of Marseille's many links with its neighboring island. (Another, less convivial link is the number of Corsicans in Marseille's police force.)

"I know what you need," said Sam. "Another coffee and a glass of *myrte.*"

They sat outside, with an uninterrupted view of the bobbing carpet of boats in the harbor, and conversation turned to Mimi and Philippe's wedding.

"It should be fun," said Elena. "I'm sure they have nice friends. I'm looking forward to it. But it's also made me think about us. I mean, how do you feel about dividing our time between here and L.A.?"

"I have to say that life here gets to you. To be honest, I haven't thought about L.A. for weeks."

"I've thought about it a lot. And I've come to realize that, for me, L.A. means work and Provence means, you know, pleasure." She looked at Sam, her face a silent question.

"That sounds to me like a pretty good reason for staying here," said Sam. "I guess I'd better get a job."

He was rewarded by the biggest smile of the evening.

The following morning, Sam joined Reboul on the terrace for breakfast.

"How was the opera?"

"Beautiful," said Reboul. "Quite beautiful. Monica was enchanted. She'll probably come downstairs singing." He poured coffee for them. "Now, then. Where were we last night?"

"You were telling me what makes Coco tick. But before we get on to that, there's another thing that's been puzzling me. These miniature hands. I mean, if she's connected to these robberies, why leave clues like that? It doesn't make sense."

"Sam, it's entirely consistent with her character. First of all, she thinks that what she does is art, and that art should be signed by the artist. The hands are her signature. She's also an extremely confident woman — confident perhaps to the point of recklessness. She would have been quite sure that nobody would pick these little details up. And, until you and Philippe came along, she was right. The police didn't notice them, and Mimi only picked up on them by accident. Even so, it's highly circumstantial evidence. If you confronted her with it, she'd laugh in your face."

Sam had to agree. "You're right. I'd thought of asking Hervé to take a look at the situation, but I guess there's no point. What can he do?"

"Don't give up," said Reboul. "If she's done it three times, there's always a good chance that she'll do it again — and that would be the moment to catch her."

While Sam was taking this in, they were joined on the terrace by Monica, a picture in black and white — white shirt, white pants, shiny black sunglasses, and shiny black hair. "You two are looking far too serious on such a lovely morning. What's the matter? Has the *rosé* finally run out?"

Claudine sat in the back of the car, going through the material she was taking to the Johnsons. There was a folder containing the paperwork that has to accompany any transaction in France. There was a selection of page proofs, complete with picture captions. And there was a detailed suggested design of the cover. This was going to be quite a coup for the magazine, she thought, as Roland, her driver, pulled up at the gates of the Johnson house.

"Did you remember to bring the biscuits?" Claudine had been warned by Philippe that they were likely to be met on the drive by Percy, and that he had a weakness for attacking strange cars.

"But of course, madame," said Roland. "The very best — the bone-shaped Fido biscuit. I have a box of them here."

Sure enough, Percy appeared as they were going up the drive, but he quickly abandoned all thoughts of an attack as he was showered with a handful of biscuits. Johnson was watching with interest from the front door, and was smiling as he greeted Claudine.

"Well, you certainly know the way to a dog's heart. Come on in."

"Divine," said Claudine, as they went through the house to Johnson's office. "Even more gorgeous than I expected."

"That's the spirit. I can see we're going to get on famously. Now let's have a look at what you've brought."

Claudine began to spread the proofs across Johnson's desk, starting with the cover, a long shot of the house, glowing in the sunlight, under the headline "Paradise for Sale."

Johnson nodded. "I like that," he said. "Jolly good."

His enthusiasm increased as Claudine took him through the six pages of the article, ending with a small space, blank except for a question mark. "Here I need your help," said Claudine. "For people who would like to know more — and I'm sure there will be many — we should have the name and contact details of someone who can give them more information: the price, obviously, and anything else you think would interest a prospective buyer. But I'm sure you don't want to do that yourself."

"No problem. I have this lawyer chappie in Nice. Very sound man. His office can take care of that. This is all most satisfactory. I have just one question. How much would I owe you for all this?"

"*Mais rien du tout.* Nothing. You are providing the magazine with a marvelous story. If your house sells because of the article, a case of Champagne, perhaps. But that's all."

Johnson did some simple calculations. A real estate agent's commission would be around five percent. On a sale of ten million, that would be half a million euros he wouldn't have to pay. "Excellent," he said. "Every little bit helps."

Chapter 22

Ah, the joys of entertaining.

The Fitzgerald house was being transformed for the party that would take place the following evening. Workmen were putting up the white canvas awnings around the terraces. Three men with musical credentials were assembling the miniature bandstand, and deliveries seemed to be arriving every five minutes: Trois Étoiles Chez Vous, the most fashionable catering company on the coast, had organized tablecloths, napkins, and cutlery, and a supply of every kind of intoxicating liquid, from Champagne to beer. Three dozen *flambeaux,* the flaming torches that were an indispensable part of Riviera parties, were being installed at strategic points along the drive and around the garden. And then there was a fusillade of phone calls, principally from the florists, who were dithering about the correct balance between orchids and lilies.

In the midst of it all was Kathy. She had been joined by Coco, who had volunteered to act as interpreter and second in command. Fitz had, very wisely, locked himself in his office until the dust settled.

Kathy pushed the hair from her eyes and drew a deep breath. "I don't know what I'd have done without you," she said to Coco. "You've been terrific."

"I've enjoyed it," said Coco. "The house is going to look wonderful. Now tell me — what are you going to wear? The men will all be in dinner jackets."

Before Kathy could reply, the phone rang yet again. It was Philippe, who was in Nice, asking if he and Mimi could come by for one last look at the arrangements. "Sure you can," said Kathy, by now almost giddy with pre-party anticipation. "Come on over."

By a happy coincidence, when they arrived half an hour later the last of the *flambeaux* were being placed along each side of the drive, and Mimi hopped out of the car to take a quick shot. "These will look sensational at night when they're lit." Then she took another shot, this time of Kathy, who was walking up the drive to meet them.

"Absolutely not for publication," said Kathy, with a smile. "My hair's a total mess. Now, where shall we start?"

They toured the terraces. They admired the bandstand, the long dinner table, the placing of smaller tables and chairs around the pool, with Mimi making notes or taking shots of promising locations.

As they were leaving, Philippe asked Kathy, "What time would you like us to get here this evening?"

"Listen," said Kathy, "as far as Fitz and I are concerned, you're two of our guests, and we want you to enjoy the evening — pre-dinner drinks, dinner, dancing, the works. I just know the other guys are going to love you."

"Well," said Mimi, "this place is a photographer's dream. I think you'll be pleased. This is going to be one of those evenings we call 'suitable for framing.' "

On their way back to Marseille, Mimi and Philippe compared this with their recent experience of eating in the hotel kitchen at the Sofitel. "You've met more Americans than I have," said Mimi. "Are they all like that — you know, generous and so enthusiastic?"

"I think so," said Philippe. "It must be something in the genes. They make some of us Europeans look like a pretty sad bunch. Anyway, it's going to be a good evening, I think. Let's stop off and see Elena and Sam — tell them to be on their best behavior."

They found Elena and Sam at their new house, in a state of mild euphoria. All the kitchen equipment had just been installed, and they were playing with the appliances like a couple of children with a bunch of new toys.

"Isn't this great?" said Elena. "It might even get Sam to take up cooking."

Sam was scratching his head over a manual that described the joys of using a ceramic hob to prepare his culinary triumphs. "Not a chance," he said cheerfully. "I'll never figure out how all these damn things work."

But Elena wasn't going to let him off the hook. "I'm going to have Alphonse come over. He'll explain everything." She turned to Mimi. "How did you get on at the Fitzgeralds'?"

"Very good. It would be difficult to take a bad shot there. It's a marvelous setting, and they've decorated it beautifully. Coco has done a great job."

At the mention of Coco's name, Sam looked up from his manual. "She's over there a lot, isn't she?"

"Kathy says she's a godsend."

We'll see, thought Sam. We'll see.

■ ■ ■ ■

The morning of the party saw Kathy up early, looking for any signs of unsettled weather. But the sky was deep blue, with only two small cotton-ball clouds fighting a losing battle with the rising sun. Greatly relieved, she saw that this was going to be one of the three hundred days of sunshine promised each year by the tourist board.

She set off on yet another check of the preparations. The awnings were perfect, the little bandstand quite charming, the tables and chairs around the pool arranged just so, the *flambeaux,* even unlit, promising to look spectacular. She consulted the list that had been her constant companion for the past several days: just three last-minute arrivals — the caterer with the food, the florist, and the hairdresser Coco had organized for the houseguests — were scheduled for today. It was all going according to plan.

Six thirty on a glorious evening, and the advance party had already arrived. Kathy had asked Elena, Mimi, Philippe, and Sam to come early, and they were having a drink on the terrace with Coco. They made an elegant group: Coco and Elena in their best long dresses, Mimi in her black silk frock coat and white silk pants, Philippe in a white dinner jacket, and Sam, who disliked dressing up, in what he called undertaker's black.

"Coco, I'm impressed," said Elena. "With all you have going on, how did you manage to do so much for Kathy?"

"Oh, it was a pleasure — much easier than dealing with a bunch of temperamental workmen. Although I must say they did a good job on your kitchen. I hope you're pleased."

"Thrilled," said Elena. "I'm going to buy Sam a chef's hat to celebrate."

The reluctant chef was quick to change the subject. "Tell us about the other guests."

"I think you'll like them. They're amusing, and they love parties. It should be a very pleasant evening, as long as I can keep Hubert from joining the musicians."

"Why's that?"

"He tries to sing, and it's terrible." Coco shuddered. "Like a frog croaking."

The sound of suppressed giggling and the clatter of high heels announced the arrival of Kathy, Fitz, and their six houseguests. The ladies were resplendent, with diamonds everywhere — necklaces and earrings, brooches and bracelets.

"Putain!" said Philippe to Sam, in a whisper. "It looks like a Cartier sales convention."

Mimi was already organizing the ladies into a glittering group in front of their husbands, ensuring that everyone had a glass of Champagne and the widest possible smile.

She was still taking the "just one more" shot that photographers can never resist when the other guests started to arrive. Armand and Edouard, the gay couple who worked in one of the big Paris fashion houses, were first, both in white suits with matching red carnations in their buttonholes. They were obviously friendly with the next arrival, the ageless Nina de Montfort, accompanied by her latest young admirer, and there was a minor explosion of air kisses and compliments.

Coco, of course, was the only one who knew everybody, and she was in charge of making the introductions, followed closely by Philippe, who was busy putting names to faces.

Some were easier than others. For instance, the polo-playing Alain Laffont, tall, dark, and thirsty, and the equally statuesque Stanislavska, were not a pair one could forget. But Coco's new clients, the Osbornes, although young and pleasant, were in no way memorable. Hubert, the cosmetic surgeon crooner, and his wife, the wrinkle-free Eloise, had a certain bizarre charm. And finally there was Coco's father, Alex, suave and deeply tanned.

Coco had asked Elena and Sam to circulate, and Sam made at once for Alex Dumas. "Hi," he said. "I'm Sam, one of Coco's satisfied clients. You must come around and see what she's done for us. How long are you down here for?"

Alex smiled and shrugged. "Not long, unfortunately. But I come down to see her quite often. Maybe during my next visit? How about you? I hope you'll have time to enjoy your house."

While Sam was getting the measure of Alex, Elena had been chatting to Armand and Edouard, who had immediately made a good impression.

"What a fabulous dress," said Edouard. "Where did *that* come from?"

"Not Paris, I'm afraid. It was a little place in L.A."

"Do you know, I thought so," said Armand. "Americans are *so* good with bosoms." He kissed his fingertips, and Elena could feel herself blushing.

Fitz had moved in on Alex to renew the

acquaintance that had begun in Paris, and Sam had taken his empty glass to the bar, where he was suddenly joined by Nina de Montfort, eyelashes aflutter as she looked him up and down.

"Where have *you* been hiding?"

CHAPTER 23

Elena was not amused. "Sam Levitt, I was watching you with that woman. What did you think you were doing?"

"Mingling, my sweet. Kathy told me to mingle, and I was mingling."

"You had your arm around her waist."

"Mimi's fault. She wanted to take a picture of us. I could hardly stand six feet away. So relax. You know that I am forever a slave to your charms."

"I know that you're full of it. But if you get me a drink I'll forgive you."

They stood at the bar, watching the crowd. Hubert had persuaded Mimi to take a selfie of the two of them. Nina was now having a very intimate conversation with Alain, the polo player. The American guests seemed to have established an *entente cordiale* with the French. Coco and Kathy were doing the rounds from group to group. The atmosphere was convivial, with plenty of laughter. It looked as though Coco's prediction of an amusing evening was coming true.

Kathy called for everybody's attention by climbing up on the bandstand and waving her arms. "OK, everyone — it's time we gave you something to eat. Follow me."

She led the way over to the west terrace, where name cards had been provided for each place. To his relief, Sam found that he was seated between two of the houseguests, a safe distance from Nina de Montfort. Elena was also pleased when she found that she would be sitting between Armand and Edouard, with the promise of some indiscreet fashion gossip. When everyone was seated, Mimi asked them all to raise their glasses toward the camera, and she took a few quick shots.

Kathy took over to make a short speech of welcome, which ended with heartfelt thanks to Coco for all her help. "Not only all this," she said, waving an arm at the table, the flowers, and the other decorations, "but she even fixed us up for a weekend on the beach in Saint-Tropez. What a girl! Please join me in a toast to my friend and guardian angel, Coco Dumas."

Conversation resumed, and dinner was served, a light summer banquet: chilled Green Zebra gazpacho, cold lobster on basil linguine, and, for homesick Americans, chocolate cheesecake. As coffee was served, the band on the other side of the house could be heard getting into their first number, an upbeat version of *La Mer.*

Some guests stayed, chatting at the table; others drifted off toward the music. Sam guided Elena onto the tiny dance floor, where they could catch up on how they spent dinner.

"Those two guys," said Elena. "They're scandalous. You have no idea what goes on in those Parisian fitting rooms."

"Do I want to?"

"Probably not. How was your dinner?"

"Fine. Two very nice women, and you'll be pleased to hear I didn't lay a hand on either of them. *Ouch!*"

"Sorry. Was that your foot?"

Other couples had joined them on the floor. Fitz, a latter-day Fred Astaire, was gliding Stanislavska around the floor, and Alain was doing the same with Kathy. Nina and her young admirer, Hubert and Mrs. Hoffman, each couple was exhibiting its ballroom techniques, with Mimi flitting among them. The reaction of dancers to the camera varied — the more adventurous men bending their partners backward, the others smiling or waving. Nina had taken a rose from the vase on her table and tucked it into her cleavage before posing for Mimi.

The dance floor had filled up, and Elena and Sam were taking a break. They noticed that Coco's father was dancing with his daughter, hardly moving and deep in conversation, when they were distracted by the sight of Hubert making his way in a determined fashion toward the bandstand. Coco, fearing an outbreak of singing, left her father, swooped on Hubert, and twirled him into the middle of the floor. Her deserted dad shrugged, smiled, and came over to join Elena and Sam.

"Poor Coco," said Elena. "Does she have to do that often?"

"I don't think she minds. She'd rather do that than have him sing. Are you both having a pleasant evening?"

Sam nodded. "I think everybody is, largely thanks to Coco. She's really worked hard. I hope she gets a little rest in Saint-Tropez."

Alex shook his head. "Unfortunately, we both have to be in Paris for a meeting on Monday. One of my friends has bought a place near here and Coco has some ideas to show him." He looked across the dance floor. "I see she's managed to get Hubert away from the band — I'd better go and help her guide him to the bar."

With a final flourish of the guitar, the music had stopped, to be replaced by a roll of the drums. Stanislavska, who had been a frequent visitor to the bar, was standing in the middle of the floor, one arm raised. Slowly, she bent forward and took hold of the hem of her long dress. More drumrolls as, inch by inch, she pulled the dress up to her hips and kicked off her shoes.

"Is this the cabaret?" said Sam.

"Well, I don't think she's going to sing."

She didn't. Instead, she performed a slow-motion split to a rapt, mainly masculine audience. One last drumroll, and she was finished, her head bowed down. There was a brief silence, and then a burst of applause as she stood up, bowed, picked up her shoes, and sauntered off the floor.

"Well, that definitely beats singing," said Sam. "What do you think she does for an encore?"

A few minutes after midnight, Mimi and Sam were talking to Kathy when they saw a car coming down the driveway. Mimi started checking her camera.

Sam was squinting into the headlights as the car pulled up. "This is a hell of a time to arrive at a party."

225

Kathy smiled. "These aren't guests. It's the security service. Great guys — they come by every hour all through the night." She turned to Mimi. "I'm sure they'd love a picture." She beckoned them to get out of the car.

Mimi placed the men on the side of the driveway between two of the *flambeaux.* *"Alors,"* she said. "Look fierce."

The two men put on their sunglasses, puffed out their chests, scowled, and folded their arms. "Perfect," said Mimi. "I'll give the shots to Madame Fitzgerald."

By the time they had rejoined the party, it was beginning to wind down. The band was playing one slow, romantic tune after another, and it was time for the first farewells. Once again the night air was filled with the sound of air kisses, murmured vows of friendship, and the exchange of invitations to lunches and dinners that often mark the last moments of a successful party.

But for Fitz, the evening wasn't over. He had raided his private bar and found a 1936 Cognac that he said would be the only fitting way to end the day. His exhausted houseguests declined, having already had too much of a good thing, and so they left Fitz with Kathy, Mimi, Elena, Philippe, and Sam.

The *flambeaux* were flickering, the moon was up, the scent of the flowers as smooth and intoxicating as the Cognac; it was one of those rare moments of shared well-being, and there was a long, contented silence, finally broken by Fitz.

"Great evening," he said. "I thought all you girls looked terrific." He looked over at Kathy and winked. "Good to see all those jewels get an outing."

"Certainly was," said Sam. "That was quite a display." He took a thoughtful sip of Cognac. "I hope you won't mind my saying this, but I wouldn't recommend that you take them down to Saint-Tropez. There have been one or two incidents on the coast with hotel safes that weren't too safe."

Kathy was nodding. "You're so right. That's why I've told the girls, we'll all have to make do with beach jewelry, and leave the Sunday-best stuff here. Fitz had this safe installed — it's as big as a coffin, with a door six inches thick. Plus, there are those security guys. Anyone tries to break in, they're here in two minutes. So I think we'll be fine."

"Good," said Sam. "Oh, before I forget. There's a great beach restaurant not far from where you'll be staying, Le Club 55.

Very informal — you can have lunch in your bikini."

Fitz grinned, and patted his stomach. "I'll bear that in mind."

CHAPTER 24

Sam and Reboul had fallen into the agreeable habit of having breakfast together, when they would gossip like two Marseille fishwives about what they had been doing and whom they had met. This morning, the day after the party, there was no shortage of suitable subjects: Nina de Montfort's cleavage; Stanislavska's memorable split; Hubert, the frustrated crooner; the stunning display of diamonds worn by Kathy and her houseguests; and the decision to leave the jewels in an empty house during the weekend.

"It's all making me think my hunch is right," said Sam. "Coco arranged the weekend in Saint-Tropez but said she couldn't come with them. And another thing — she seems to have a very close relationship with her father, and it wouldn't surprise me if he were somehow involved. It's always good to have an accomplice you can trust."

Reboul looked up, his croissant halfway to

his mouth. "What would he do? Hold her handbag while she was opening safes?"

"I don't know. But somebody has to get rid of the diamonds."

"So what are you going to do? Tell Hervé? I don't think he'll get too excited about a hunch."

"I know that. But I have an idea. If we can catch her with the jewels, that should be enough for Hervé."

"Who's 'we'?"

"Me — at first, anyway. But I'll need some police help."

"Hmm. Well, OK. You get your idea ready, and I'll call Hervé."

"Could you ask him for a favor?"

"I already am. What is it now?"

"Could he run a check on Alex Dumas?"

That evening, Hervé seemed to be in a mood to indulge Sam — helped, no doubt, by a glass of Marseille's best *pastis* and one of Havana's finest cigars. "Alright, Sam. I'm ready to be amused. What is this idea?"

"I guess I should explain how I got there. First, those three unsolved robberies were all carried out in houses that Coco Dumas had renovated, and none of them showed any signs of unlawful entry — no tampering with the alarm systems, no forcing of any doors, not even any fingerprints. This means, obviously, that the thief had all the necessary keys and codes. Coco had been in a position, one way or another, to get these. She ordered all the security equipment and she supervised its installation. She might even have set the codes herself — just another detail her clients didn't have to worry about; or perhaps she said she needed the codes in case her clients forgot them."

Sam paused to take a drink. Hervé watched him, a half-smile on his face, as though he were enjoying the entertainment. "Carry on, Sam. Carry on."

"OK, so we now come to what I'm convinced will be the next robbery, the Fitzgerald house, which Coco also renovated. Why? Three reasons: thanks to her, the house will be empty over the weekend; next, she turned down an invitation to go with the Fitzgeralds and their guests; and finally, as I saw at the party last night, the amount of jewelry on display was enough to stock a boutique. And it will all be left in the house."

Hervé, still smiling, said, "So what is this idea?"

"I'd like to stake out the house. When I see Coco go in, I call the police — someone recommended by you — and ask them to meet me at the Negresco, where we pick up Coco and the jewels."

Hervé had started to shake his head. "Why wait? Why not pick her up coming out of the house?"

"Because if I'm right about her father being involved, she'll be going back to the Negresco, where he's staying. And if he's part of the crime, we need to catch him as well."

Hervé was now looking thoughtful. He reached into a pocket and took out a folded sheet of paper. "These are the results of the check we did on Alex Dumas." He pushed the paper across the table to Sam. "There's something in there that I have to say would fit your story. The last paragraph, down at the bottom."

Sam found the paragraph under the heading "Business Interests," which included real estate in Thailand and New York, a share of a lumber company in Canada, and "various directorships" of firms in Antwerp.

"Antwerp?" said Sam. "That's where old diamonds go for facelifts."

"Exactly," said Hervé. "Recut, repolished, reidentified, just like new. And a great many of them. More than $16 billion worth of polished diamonds go through the Antwerp exchanges every year."

"And Alex Dumas does business there."

Hervé grinned. "I thought you might be interested. Now listen, Sam. I think you might have something. But I can't take the case over — it's not my turf. What I can do is arrange for you to meet my young friend Angus Laffitte — Capitaine Laffitte, to give him his proper title — who's based in Nice. If you can convince him, I'm sure he'll give you what you want. I'll call him this evening and get back to you with the time."

"Angus? Is that a usual name in Nice?"

"Scottish mother."

Lying in bed later, Sam and Elena were having what Sam had come to think of as one of their frozen moments. He had been full of excitement that Hervé had been convinced. But Elena had listened to his account with a stony face, and when he had mentioned the possible involvement of Alex Dumas, she had turned on him. "Anyone else you think might be involved? Francis? Mimi and Philippe? This whole thing is ridiculous. Give it up. Get a life."

"I know you like Coco. So do I. But you have to admit that it looks pretty bad for her. Anyway, I'm nearly there. The crunch comes this weekend. So bear with me, OK?"

Elena's answer was a snort of disdain, and she turned her back to him. They both slept poorly that night.

Sam was up early the next morning, and on the *autoroute* leading to Nice before the sun was fully up. His appointment with Laffitte wasn't until eleven o'clock, so he'd have time for breakfast and what he hoped would be a reconciliation with Elena over the phone.

Breakfast, on the terrace of a quiet café overlooking the sea, was a pleasure. The attempted reconciliation was not. Elena's voice was chilly and distant from the moment she picked up the phone. This nonsense had become an obsession, she said. Even worse, he was targeting someone whom Elena considered a friend. How could he do that? But before he had a chance to defend himself, she said, "I don't want to talk about it," and hung up.

Sam ordered a second coffee, and pondered the ups and downs of their relationship. From past experience, if he was proved to be right he knew that Elena would accept it, and might even apologize. If not, he could expect a severe scolding followed by several frigid days and lonely nights — one more reason why he'd better not be wrong.

The office of Capitaine Laffitte was in the

Commissariat Central de Police, an imposing blockhouse on the Avenue Maréchal Foch. Laffitte was also imposing — a big, broad-shouldered man with a military haircut and a handshake like a vice. His voice came as a surprise: perfect English softened by a Scottish accent.

"Sit yourself down, laddie, and tell me all about it. Hervé's given me the general idea, but the devil is in the details. I want to hear everything."

For the next half hour, Sam went through what he knew and what he thought was going to happen. Laffitte paid close attention, making notes and asking occasionally for clarification. When Sam had finished, Laffitte sat back in his chair, a frown of concentration on his face.

"Very good," he said. "I just have one wee question. If your theory is correct, when do you think she'll make her move?"

"It has to be tomorrow. The Fitzgeralds are leaving tomorrow morning to go to Saint-Tropez. The Dumas are leaving on Sunday for Paris, which gets them conveniently out of the way when the robbery is discovered. That leaves Saturday. During the day, the gardener and the maid will be there, so it has to be Saturday night."

"Which means we don't have much time."

Laffitte reached for his phone. "Can you come back this afternoon? I'm going to need a couple more bodies, and I'd like you to be there when I brief them."

Sam used the time to check in at the Hôtel Westminster, on the Promenade des Anglais, and have a quick lunch at a small beach restaurant. He was starting to feel nervous. Laffitte seemed to be confident, and now there was no going back. Coco *had* to turn up.

Laffitte thought there was every chance that she would; indeed, he was beginning to count on it. If he could be the officer who solved three perfect robberies, and prevented a fourth, his future would look very bright — maybe he'd even get a promotion to commandant. He looked at his watch. The two men he had chosen would arrive any minute, and so would Sam, he was sure. Americans were always punctual.

They arrived almost together, and Sam was introduced to René and Marc, two burly, keen-looking young men with regulation military haircuts.

They greeted Sam in English, and were amused when he expressed surprise. "Everyone in Nice speaks a little English," said Marc. "It's good for business."

The three of them sat down in front of

Laffitte's desk, and he began his briefing, going through all that Sam had told him before moving on to what he called the fun and games of Saturday night.

"I'll go to the house with Sam. When we see her come out, I'll call you. That'll give you plenty of time to get over to the Negresco. Stay well away from the entrance, on the opposite side of the road, and wait for us there. When we arrive, we'll have a wee meeting with the night manager; I want him to come up to her apartment with us. I'll have a warrant if he needs persuading. Once we have the jewels, we pick up the father and off we go. OK? Any questions?"

"What about equipment?" René asked. "Firearms?"

Laffitte laughed and shook his head "Nothing like that. We'll have binoculars, and you should have handcuffs. But that's about it."

Sam went back to the Westminster that evening, suddenly feeling exhausted. It had been a long, trying day. He thought about calling Elena, but decided he couldn't take another dose of disapproval, so he found the hotel bar, had two large Scotches, and went to bed.

■ ■ ■ ■

He slept late, and he was still half asleep on his way to the shower before he started to think about the robbery. Tonight was the night, and it promised to be a day that would strain his patience. He ordered breakfast and the newspaper. He sat out on the terrace of his room and stared at the sunlight on the sea. He called Elena's number and left a message on her voice mail. When midday finally arrived, he called the hotel in Saint-Tropez to make sure that the Fitzgeralds and their guests had arrived. He watched CNN until he could take no more bad news. And he looked at his watch, again and again, only to find that the hands seemed to be stuck.

Finally, it was 10:00 p.m., time to meet Laffitte in the hotel lobby. He had abandoned his uniform for dark pants and a windbreaker. A pair of binoculars hung around his neck, and Sam caught a glimpse of the handcuffs attached to his belt.

"En forme?" said Laffitte. "It's a perfect night for robbers — no moon, and plenty of cloud cover. Shall we go?"

They got into a small, unmarked car for the short drive to Cap Ferrat, with Sam showing the way to the Fitzgerald house. They drove past the entrance, around a bend, and parked in a thick pool of shadow. Walking back to the house, Laffitte stopped to try out his binoculars. "Pretty good," he said. "German army issue, infrared night vision. We shouldn't have any trouble recognizing her. Now we need to find somewhere to wait."

By now, they had almost reached the entrance gates, and with a grunt of satisfaction Laffitte stepped off the narrow road. "See those oleanders? They'll be fine." They pushed their way into the middle of the clump, the leafy branches closing behind them. They would be invisible from the other side of the road.

And then started the hard part — the wait. A car passed, the music from its radio hanging in the air for a few seconds before silence returned. They saw movement farther up the road: an elderly Labrador, doing its evening rounds.

Just after 10:30, they were jolted alert by the sight of a small van pulling into the entrance, going up the driveway, and parking in front of the main double doors. Two men got out, both with lit flashlights. "The security guys," said Sam. "I was told they come by every hour."

The men separated, each taking a different side of the house, and set off around the back, toward the pool area, before rejoining one another by the van and driving off. The entire visit was over in less than five minutes.

The night was very still, and Sam was starting to have doubts. "Relax," said Laffitte. "She's got all night."

Half an hour passed, and then they heard the sound of a car coming around the bend, slowing down, and turning into the entrance. It was a black Fiat 500, the most welcome sight Sam had seen all day; he recognized Coco's car from her many visits to their house in Marseille. "That's her," he said. Laffitte had his binoculars trained on the car as a female arm appeared and the entry code was tapped in. The gates swung open, and the Fiat drove up to the house and parked in the shadows. Coco got out, unlocked the front door, and disappeared inside the house.

"Quel culot," said Laffitte. "What a nerve! Suppose someone sees her?"

"Knowing her," said Sam, "I'm sure she'll have thought of that."

She had. On her cell phone was a message from Kathy Fitzgerald asking her to drop by and check in on the house when she had time. In fact, the message was left from Paris just before Kathy and Fitz came down, but Coco had arranged to have any mention of the date doctored and made inaudible. The message was timeless.

Laffitte had his binoculars up again, searching for any signs of light or movement, but the house remained dark and still. "At least she's careful indoors," said Laffitte. "I have a feeling this part won't take too long."

Sam checked his watch. Coco had been in the house for eight minutes. Another five minutes went by before the front door opened and Coco got into her car and drove down the driveway and through the gateway, pausing to check that the gate had closed behind her before she turned into the road.

"So far so good," said Laffitte, taking out his phone and tapping in a number as they walked back to their car. "Marc? It looks as though she's done the job. She's just left the house. Keep an eye out for her car, a black Fiat 500. We'll be back in a few minutes. Everything OK? Good." He turned back to Sam. "This is the part I like best: catching them."

During the drive back, Sam resisted the unworthy temptation to call Elena, instead listening to Laffitte planning what he was

241

going to say to the hotel's night manager. "There might be some resistance," he said. "A top hotel like the Negresco doesn't like the police rushing around the corridors at night. It tends to make the guests nervous."

They pulled up and parked fifty yards past the hotel entrance. Marc and René met them as they were getting out of the car, and confirmed seeing a black Fiat 500 going into the hotel's private parking area ten minutes earlier.

The night manager, a suave and helpful young man, clearly welcomed the stimulating distraction of a police visit investigating what Laffitte described to him as "a most delicate matter." He did, however, insist that he accompany them — quoting hotel regulations — to Coco's apartment.

Coco opened the door. She was holding a glass of wine, and had kicked off her shoes, as women often do after a hard day's work. She looked at Sam with astonishment. "Sam? What are you doing here? Who are these people?"

"I'm afraid they're police. Can we come in and talk to you?"

"What about?"

Laffitte stepped forward. "Madame, we have a warrant, and we need to talk to you. Please."

"This is outrageous. But if you must come in, come in."

She stood in front of the table, hands on hips, and glared at them. "Now what?"

Laffitte sighed. "I'm sure you know why we're here. We saw you entering the Fitzgerald house on Cap Ferrat earlier this evening."

"So?"

"What were you doing there?"

"That's none of your business. But if you must know, I was doing a favor for the owners." She took out her cell phone and scrolled down to Kathy's message. "Here. Listen." She passed the phone to Laffitte, moving aside as she did so and revealing a small backpack lying on the table behind her. Sam saw that Laffitte had noticed it.

He finished listening to the message. "Do you normally do this kind of thing at night?"

Coco shrugged. "I was in Antibes all day, and then I went out to dinner. After that, I went to the house. Look, this is really unacceptable. Please go."

"Of course," said Lafitte. "Oh, before I do, perhaps you would let me see what is in that backpack."

Coco picked up the backpack, and very deliberately took out the contents: a flashlight, a box of tissues, some keys, and a pair of black cotton gloves. She turned the empty bag inside out and tossed it at Laffitte. "Satisfied?"

"You know what?" Sam whispered to Laffitte. "We're in the wrong room. She must have stopped off on the way."

Laffitte took Marc and René aside. "You stay with her here. She is not to leave this room and she is not to use the phone. Is that clear?"

Sam, Laffitte, and the night manager, who had been watching everything with bemused curiosity, went down to reception, where they confirmed that Alex Dumas was still in residence.

"This time we're not knocking," Laffitte said to the night manager. "Bring a master key."

"I couldn't do that. Hotel regulations forbid it, unless the circumstances are exceptional."

"Believe me, they are," said Laffitte. "Let's go."

In the elevator going up to the Dumas suite, Laffitte turned to Sam and winked. "Nearly there." Sam crossed his fingers.

They tiptoed across from the elevator, the key was turned, the door flung open. And there was Alex Dumas, a look of shock on his face, made grotesque by the jeweler's loupe screwed into one eye. A pile of diamonds was on the table in front of him.

Sam felt an enormous surge of relief. "Well, I'll be damned. Where did all those come from? Room service?"

CHAPTER 25

Elena's voice came down the line like a cold shower. "So you were right and I was wrong, OK?"

Sam sighed. "Sorry about that. I won't let it happen again. Look, I'll be back later today. Can we talk about it then?" There was no answer. "Elena?" But she had ended the call; it was a disappointing start to what Sam felt was going to be a disappointing day. After the elation of the previous night, with congratulations coming thick and fast from Laffitte and his men, he now had the task of passing the news on to Reboul. It could be another very uncomfortable moment, despite Reboul's feeling that Coco would do almost anything for money. This time, he thought, it was best dealt with in person.

But first, Laffitte had asked him to come to his office before returning to Marseille. Sam checked out of the hotel and stopped for coffee and a croissant before making his way to the Commissariat Central, where he found Laffitte, not surprisingly, in the best of spirits.

"Ah, there you are, Sherlock," said Laffitte, giving Sam a bear hug. "Found some more clues? Now let's see — what have I got to tell you?"

He scratched his head and shuffled some papers on his desk. "The top laddies here are delighted, as you can imagine, and so is Hervé. They'd all like to show their appreciation in due course. I'll be calling the Fitzgeralds later today to tell them the good news. And we shall be having a long chat with Dumas *père et fille* this afternoon to find out what they did with the jewels from the other three robberies. Our colleagues in Antwerp are already working on all the Dumas connections. So it promises to be an interesting day. I'll keep you posted. But before you go, I'd like to go over what you can tell me about those other three robberies."

An hour later, Sam was on his way back to Marseille, for once not looking forward to seeing Reboul. But at least the moment was delayed. It was a Sunday, and Sunday lunch at Le Pharo was a well-established ritual. Reboul would invite half a dozen friends, Alphonse would excel himself in the kitchen, and lunch would extend until well into the afternoon. Private and delicate conversations were, for the moment, out of the question.

Sam found himself sitting between Monica and Reboul's aunt Laura, who had come over from Corsica, where Sam had met her, for a weekend in the city. To Sam's relief, he saw that Elena was out of range, next to Reboul at the far end of the table.

Monica and Laura were perfect lunchtime companions, charming and amusing. The food was up to Alphonse's high standard, the wines flowed freely, and Sam began to relax. By four o'clock, when the guests had started to make their farewells, he was feeling a little more optimistic.

He waited until Reboul had said goodbye to the last guest before cornering him.

"Francis, we need to talk."

Reboul smiled, and shook his head. "Sam, do you think Elena wouldn't have told me?"

"I suppose I might have guessed. What can I say? I'm very, very sorry it turned out like this."

Reboul sighed. "As I once said to you, Coco was always obsessed with money; it was like an addiction, and I think her father's just the same. It's a great pity. She's such a talented woman. She doesn't need to steal. Of course I'm sad, but I'm not really surprised. Come with me, bring a Cognac, and tell me all about it." He led the way to a far corner of the terrace, and Sam could almost feel Elena's eyes on him.

Reboul was still shaking his head when they sat back down. "What a silly girl. I still find it hard to believe."

"Tell me, Francis — how was Elena when she told you? Sad? Angry?"

"Both. Sad because she'd lost a friend, angry at what Coco had done, and also because there's no possibility of innocence; the two of them were caught with the goods. End of story."

"You know that Elena is furious with me over this?"

Reboul smiled. "I don't think that will last long. But if I were you I would tread carefully for the next day or two. Maybe a little peace offering wouldn't hurt."

Sam's cell phone went off early the next morning. It was Kathy Fitzgerald, ecstatic with gratitude. Laffitte had told her everything. The jewels were being returned to her, under a police escort, later in the day, and Fitz had a great idea for a thank-you gift. He was already on the phone to his man in Paris to arrange delivery. Kathy would call back in the afternoon to fix a time.

Relations between Elena and Sam were edging back to normal; she had even kissed him on the nose before getting up, and he thought he had come up with the peace offering that Reboul had suggested. Life was looking a little more rosy. He decided to spread some of the happiness in Philippe's direction.

"Would you like some good news?"

"Always," said Philippe.

"We got Coco and her father *and* the jewels on Saturday night. How about that?"

"Well, congratulations — you did it. I have to say there were times when I had my doubts. You have to tell me everything."

"Before I do, here's an idea you might like: a sequel to the piece you did on the party. You know — the jewel robbery that failed. You'd have to get the Fitzgeralds' agreement, obviously, but it could be fun."

"Great. You know what might go with it? That shot Mimi took of all the ladies wearing their jewels, with the same shot side by side, over a caption that says, 'Before and After.' No jewels missing. What do you think?"

"Off you go, but don't forget to clear it

with Kathy. And you might want to give the police a nod — Capitaine Laffitte, in the Nice Commissariat."

"I'm on my way. Talk to you later."

Elena emerged from the bathroom, and gave Sam his first smile in twenty-four hours.

"I don't think I told you," she said. "Monica and I are having a girls' day out in Marseille. We'll be back in time for a drink this evening. See you then."

"I shall count the moments," said Sam, and was rewarded with his second smile of the day. Things were definitely looking up.

Once Elena had left, his first stop was the kitchen, where he spent a very productive half hour with Alphonse. From there, he took Alphonse over to the house, now free of workmen, where he spent the morning being taught how to operate the equipment: the induction hob, the streamlined multi-function cooker, the separate steam oven — all the chef's essentials that he had so carefully avoided throughout his life.

Alphonse left just before noon, and his exhausted pupil was having a restorative glass of *rosé* in the sunshine when his phone beeped. Kathy was calling back, as promised, and sounded more excited than ever. Fitz had pulled out all the stops, and express delivery was guaranteed for the following morning. Was that OK? In fact, it fitted in very well with Sam's plans. He gave Kathy the address and promised to call as soon as the delivery had been made.

His afternoon passed in a blur of activity, but by the time he left the house in the early evening he was confident that his little peace offering would put him back in Elena's good graces.

He found her back at Le Pharo, on the terrace with Monica and Reboul, looking tired but happy. The day in Marseille had been a great success. The ladies had explored, shopped, lunched, and shopped again. They had discussed their respective partners, of course, and had come to the conclusion that they were both pretty lucky.

Before dinner, there was an impromptu fashion show, with Elena and Monica modeling what they had bought, and Reboul took advantage of a changing-room break to ask Sam how what he called "the Elena situation" was going.

"It's a little easier," said Sam. "I'm hoping tomorrow should do it. Are you sure it's OK if I borrow Alphonse for an hour or so?"

Reboul grinned. "Of course. Do you want to borrow his chef's hat as well?"

■ ■ ■ ■

The following morning began with a brief negotiation over breakfast.

"I have a little surprise for you," Sam said to Elena. "I have to be out all morning, but I'll be through by lunchtime."

"Can't I come?"

"Absolutely not."

"Even if I promise to be adorable?"

"No."

This brought a pout from Elena, but it was a good-humored pout, and Sam was whistling as he left.

After a quick stop in Marseille, he arrived at the house to set up his peace offering. It was to be a homemade lunch, prepared, with a little help from Alphonse, by Sam. The menu was simple: chilled melon soup, *filet mignon* with a red wine sauce, salad with balsamic dressing, and Alphonse's most decadent chocolate tart. The wine was a favorite of Elena's, a Châteauneuf-du-Pape 2010 Vieux Télégraphe.

Sam had just started to set out the ingredients when he heard the grunt of an engine, and went out to find a delivery truck and two men. Fitz's gift had arrived — a dozen wooden boxes, which the men stacked with some reverence against the kitchen wall. Sam read the inscriptions on the boxes with mounting astonishment. Two cases of Château Lafite Rothschild. Two cases of Château Latour. Two cases of Romanée-Conti La Tâche. Two cases of Grand Cru Chablis. Two cases of Krug Champagne. And two cases of Château d'Yquem. It added up to the foundation of a truly magnificent wine cellar.

There was also an envelope containing a corkscrew and a one-word note on Fitz's writing paper: "Enjoy."

Sam called Kathy at once. She was thrilled that he was thrilled, and the conversation ended with promises to get together as soon as Sam and Elena were free. But meanwhile, there was lunch to prepare.

Sam started outside, at the small table on the terrace that he had chosen for the great event, dressing the table with accessories borrowed from Le Pharo: a thick linen tablecloth and napkins, crystal glasses, silver cutlery, and fine bone china. In the center of the table he placed the bouquet of white roses he had picked up in Marseille. He was standing back admiring his handiwork when he heard the clatter of Alphonse's van, and the chef bustled up to the table, making several tiny adjustments before turning to

Sam. "*Voilà* — now it is perfect. Come with me."

He opened the back of his van, gave Sam a large tray, and started to load it. There was a small tureen and a sealed container of melon soup, a jar containing the wine sauce, and a covered dish for the chocolate tart. "You said you would do the steak and salad yourself, yes? Here — you'll need this." He hung a long, freshly starched apron around Sam's neck.

In the kitchen, Alphonse gave Sam strict and detailed instructions about the presentation of the soup and the heating and application of the red wine sauce before wishing Sam *bon appétit* and heading back to his own kitchen.

Sam looked at his watch. He was relieved that he'd asked Olivier, the chauffeur, to bring Elena over. He needed the extra time for the finishing touches; also, he wanted her first sight of him to be in his apron. Should he have borrowed the chef's hat? Probably not. Elena wouldn't be impressed by a hat.

She arrived on the dot at 12:30. Watching from the kitchen window, Sam saw her get out of the car and look around with a puzzled expression on her face. Smoothing his apron, he put two glasses of Champagne on a small silver tray and went out to meet her.

As she saw him, her expression changed to one of amused disbelief. "I was expecting to meet Mr. Levitt. Are you new here?"

"Just helping out, madame. Just helping out. Champagne?"

They touched glasses. "Welcome home," said Sam.

Elena smiled. "Nice to be back."

After that, it was as though the old Elena had returned. She admired the table setting, loved the chilled soup, and was most impressed by Sam's handling of the steak and wine sauce. "That apron suits you," she said. "We should do this more often."

"I have to admit it wasn't totally my own work. Alphonse had a hand in it. In fact, he managed to make the next course without any help from me at all."

The chocolate tart was followed by coffee, and Sam felt he could now take off his apron. "Would you like anything else?"

Elena looked at him in silence for a moment, and then winked — a slow, inviting wink. "How about a siesta?"

ABOUT THE AUTHOR

Peter Mayle has lived in Provence, with his wife and their two dogs, for many years. He is a Chevalier in the Légion d'Honneur.